Thunder in the morning

The bombardment of Scarborough

Lynne Reed

ISBN 0 9551817 0 4

From 1 January 2006
ISBN 978 0 9551817 0 2

Cover design by BP Design, York

Prepared, printed and distributed by:
York Publishing Services Ltd
64 Hallfield Road
Layerthorpe
York
YO31 7ZQ
Tel: 01904 431213   Website: www.yps-publishing.co.uk

Author's Note

This novel is based on actual events and personally remembered incidents that took place in Scarborough on December 16th 1914.

For dramatic effect some events described took place on other dates.

Some events are completely fictitious.

This novel is dedicated to the people of Scarborough who survived the bombardment – and to those who did not.

1

As the cold misty December dawn unfurled its wispy tendrils, three menacing dark grey shapes sped silently through the slate-coloured sea towards an unsuspecting sleeping town. It was Wednesday the 16th of December 1914, the war was in its fifth month and even the most eternal optimists were reversing their opinions that it would be all over by Christmas! It was a few minutes before eight o'clock in the morning and for the majority of people the working day had just started or was about to begin.

~

The first salvo was fired without warning. In a screaming protesting cloud the seagulls rose from their cliffside nests, circled once in terror, then, in panic-stricken flight turned inland, hopefully to safety. The first shell struck an empty barracks - fortunately one battalion had been moved out the previous evening and a replacement had not yet arrived - demolishing a paint store in the grounds of the mediaeval Castle. A sheet of flame shot upwards, prematurely lighting the morning sky.

2

Three young men had just completed their early morning swim. It was a ritual that Ben Winters, Maurice Atkinson and Colin Miller practised every day, regardless of the temperature, whatever the weather. Most of their friends and colleagues thought they were crazy but nothing deterred them. To their way of thinking it was a very healthy thing to do, no-one could deny that the three young men were indeed exceptionally fit and Scarborough's popularity as a resort had been mainly due to sea bathing.

~

They saw three ships entering the bay. At first they were merely interested, as they viewed them from their permanently hired bathing machine, where they were dressing, not realising that the vessels were hostile. After all, ships and fishing boats were everyday sights in a port. The friends were almost dressed when the first volley of shells was fired, and they immediately realised they were being attacked. Hurriedly they put on the rest of their clothes and sped up the slipway to take shelter behind the sea wall in front of the Spa. Fortunately for them the missiles aimed at that side of the bay were directed at a point much higher than their hiding place, so they were relatively safe for the time being. They debated what to do.

"We should get up to the town centre and warn everybody," said Colin.

"I expect they'll know by now, I'm sure the coastguards will have been observing. They've probably already called in the Navy", replied Ben logically. The other two agreed. They decided to stay where they were for the time being as there was nothing they could do to alleviate the situation, and they may well have put themselves in danger if they moved from their temporary refuge.

3

PC Derek Hardcastle had just started his duty round; he saw the warships steam into the bay and was on his way to the coastguard station, from where he could telephone his superiors. He rushed for shelter when the Castle above him appeared to burst into flames; as he ran into the coastguards' office he felt a tingling sensation down his back.

~

"Hey up lad, you're on fire!" said coastguard Harry Edwards as he snatched Derek's smouldering cape off his back and trampled it on the floor, putting out the flames before they could take hold. Derek was not injured: the only damage was to his cape, which was now covered in tiny scorched holes. As the three young swimmers had surmised the ships had already been observed. Dick Philips, Harry's colleague, had telephoned to the wireless station on Falsgrave moor behind the town and reported:

"Some strange ships are approaching from the north. I cannot make out what they are. They do not answer my signals. I believe they may be hostile." A few seconds later he sent a more urgent message:

"They are German warships! They are firing on us!" Then the line went completely dead as a shell cut the wires and destroyed their line of communication.

"Bugger it!" swore Dick, adding laconically, "I think we're in for a bit of a rum do."

"Well, I'd best be off," said Derek, "I'll be needed, I expect. Thanks for putting out the fire." With a wave he left the coastguards to maintain their watch and resumed his beat. Now that their lines of communication had been cut, they could only watch and wait, but Dick was sure the message would have been received at the wireless station before the line went dead, and would already have been relayed to the War Office and the Admiralty. Nevertheless, leaving Harry on watch, he cycled down to the Police station to use their telephone to make certain.

4

Iris Appleby snuggled down in the soft feather bed; "I'll get up *now*!" she said, and didn't move. The bed was so snug and warm, the bedroom so cold. It was her parents' big double bed, but her father, a merchant seaman, was away on a long voyage to Buenos Aires, her brother Mark was with him. Although Iris missed her father when he was away for so long, she enjoyed being allowed to share her mother's large bed with its high brass bedstead, so comfortable and luxuriant compared to her own single one with its iron bedstead and flock mattress. Her mother had called her three times already; it was a ritual they went through almost every morning.

"Iris, are you up yet?" came her mother's shrill voice from the bottom of the stairs.

"Nearly" called back Iris.

"Nearly? Nearly? What do you mean nearly? How can you be *nearly* up? Either you are or you aren't."

They had a similar shouted conversation almost every day, so Iris didn't bother answering, she stuck one foot out of bed thus, in her own mind, justifying that she was "nearly" up

~

Suddenly, a loud explosion rent the air followed immediately by another, then another. Iris was out of bed quicker than she'd ever moved in her life and before the echoes of the first shell had died away she was downstairs. She reached the sanctuary of the kitchen as her brother Matthew came rushing in through the back door.

"There's three warships int' harbour," he said breathlessly. "They're shelling us," he added unnecessarily, as another burst of heavy gunfire was heard.

"It's Germans! They're invading us," shrieked Mrs Appleby; she opened the cellar door and bundled her son and daughter down the steps so roughly that Iris managed to save herself from falling only by clinging to the narrow rail fixed to the wall. They settled themselves in the cellar as best they could and waited for the invasion.

5

Jimmy Dean hurriedly finished dressing; he had been warned several times about being late on duty. He'd had a final warning only yesterday and he couldn't afford to be late again. Not only would he lose his job but also his accommodation. He was a waiter at the prestigious Grand Hotel and though his wage was not munificent, his board and lodging were free. When the hotel was busy during the summer season he often made more than his weekly wage in tips. It was now, of course a very quiet time of year, being midwinter. There were at present only two permanent guests in the hotel, plus a couple of commercial travellers who were just passing through. However little he could afford, Jimmy sent home as much money as possible to his family who lived in a little colliery village in County Durham. His mother although crippled with arthritis took in other peoples' washing for a few shillings a week. His father at forty-five was slowly dying, his lungs clogged with the coal dust he had been inhaling for more than thirty years working down the pits. It would be disastrous for the whole family if Jimmy were to lose this job. He hurried out of his attic bedroom slamming the door behind him. The crash that followed was out of all proportion to the emphatic closing of the door. Very gingerly Jimmy tried to open it again: there seemed to be something blocking it. He gave a sharp shove; the door gave enough for him to see the shambles that was his room. Until then Jimmy's mind had not registered the bombardment, so intent was he in getting to the dining room on time, but he realised he'd been hearing the sound of gunfire for several minutes.

"Jesus! It looks as if a bomb's hit it!" he said aloud, and realising that's exactly what had happened, he laughed hysterically. He stopped laughing abruptly as it dawned on him that two more seconds in that room and he would have been part of the debris. Trembling, he hurried downstairs to the dining room. All the staff seemed to arrive at the same time: they were crowded into the doorway, looking aghast at the shambles that had until a few minutes ago been an elegant restaurant. All the windows, except one, had been blown in; the crockery, which had been neatly arranged on the sideboards, was all smashed, as was some of the furniture. In fact the only item that was still intact was a decanter full of wine, standing incongruously in the middle of a table surrounded by debris.

~

The manager and the headwaiter arrived together; they pushed their way through the press of people into the dining room.

"Bloody Hell!" said Peter Jones, the headwaiter. To the guests he was Pierre; he used a pseudo French accent when he addressed them, although he'd never been out of England, in fact he had never even set foot out of Yorkshire! In this moment of stress he reverted to his usual Yorkshire accent. He took in the scene very quickly.

"Well don't just stand there" he ordered the bemused staff, "there are guests coming for breakfast any minute." He issued orders, which were carried out extremely quickly and efficiently. When the guests came down for breakfast less than an hour later, they were directed to the small lounge at the north side of the building, from where they could see the rival hotel at the opposite side of the road, and the rear of the Town Hall. There was a gaping hole in the upper floors of the Royal Hotel, and the large Town Hall windows overlooking the gardens had all been blown in. In spite of the damage and inconvenience at the Grand the guests were in no way deprived of the excellent service that had contributed to the hotel's reputation.

6

Albert Bell was nearly halfway through his first delivery of the morning mail when he heard the first salvo. Thick black smoke filled the air and drifted inland, mingling with the grey morning mist and making visibility difficult in parts. When more shells followed, Albert realised that the town was being bombarded, and wondered whether to carry on with his deliveries or to return to the Post Office. It didn't take much deliberating; he decided to finish his round as usual, it would be as hazardous going back into town as it would be carrying on. He was just about to take the mail to "Dunollie", the big house where Margaret Kennedy worked as a parlour maid. They were walking out together, but as Margaret had only one half day a week and one Sunday a month off, their time together was limited. However, every morning, even though strictly speaking it wasn't one of her duties, Margaret came to the front door to take in the letters. They had a few stolen moments of privacy on the doorstep, then Albert went around the back of the house to the kitchen, for a welcome break. Cook always had a cup of strong tea and some hot buttered toast waiting for him. Albert was ready for something to eat by the time he reached "Dunollie." He started his day at about four o'clock in the morning. Margaret would join him in the kitchen after she'd sorted the morning post, she also, would be ready for a break as were the rest of the staff. They all rose early to perform their various duties, so that everything was shipshape for Sir Robert and Lady Dorothea Brent when they came down to start their day. Actually on this particular morning Sir Robert had already left the house to catch an early train to London, where he had a business meeting. Lady Dorothea did not usually rise until half way through the morning. She always breakfasted in her room on a lightly boiled egg, with thinly sliced bread and butter and a cup of weak tea. Margaret was the only one able to cut the bread almost wafer thin and completely straight, no-one else could do it with such precision.

~

Albert handed some post to two men standing talking outside a short row of shops.

"This is a rum do, Albert," said Mr Firth, as he gave a cursory glance at the two letters he'd taken from the postman. "I was in two minds whether to open up or not, but George thinks there's no point in staying shut," he nodded towards his companion, who had the tailors shop next door to his stationers.

"Aye," said George Crowther dryly, "why give t'buggers the satisfaction of thinking they're putting us out of business."

"Hardly that George, we'd not be shutting forever," Leonard Firth chuckled.

"Aye, well" was the dry reply.

"Well I'd best be getting on, there's still a lot of letters left to deliver," said Albert as he moved off.

"Don't let *us* keep you lad, she'll be waiting for you all eager like," Len called cheerfully, as Albert disappeared round the next corner. He and George chuckled; they knew about Albert's practice of breaking his round at "Dunollie," and often good-naturedly chaffed him about it. Albert took it all in good part.

~

Margaret was watching for him and opened the door before Albert had time to raise his hand to the big brass knocker.

"What's going on Albert? What's all that banging? It's not thunder."

"Nay lass, it's Germans! There's some warships int' bay, they're firing shells at us," Albert said matter-of-factly, as if it were an every day occurrence, successfully hiding his own apprehension. He didn't want to frighten Margaret, although he felt very scared himself.

"Oh My God!" Margaret screamed, as without warning a shell went through the library window at the side of the house, a few feet from where they were standing

She flung herself at Albert who put his arms around her and held her tightly. They neither saw nor heard the next shell as it hit the front of the house. They died instantaneously, together, locked in each other's arms.

George Crowther and Leonard Firth had just turned to go into their respective shops when the next barrage came.

"It's getting a bit too close for comfort, it'll probably be safer inside" said Len as he took his shop keys out of his waistcoat pocket. The next shell hit them a fraction of a second later. They were both dead before George had time to form a reply.

7

Old Walter Slack, commonly known as "Nutty", for obvious reasons, was just leaving the coal yard, his cart laden, for the start of his morning deliveries. His horse, aptly named Plodder, because of his tendency to take his time, trotted placidly down the road. Nutty loosely held the reins: he didn't need to guide the old horse Plodder knew where to go. The sudden loud bang and the sight of the flames on the Castle Hill terrified poor Plodder and he galloped as he'd never galloped before in his life. In fact until then his fastest speed had been a rarely reached steady canter.

"WHOA!" bawled Walter, "WHOA!" but the horse ignored him and carried on his headlong flight.

"Stop, yer daft bugger, allt' bloody coal's falling off. Will yer stop, yer bloody great piece of catsmeat!"

Tommy Collins, just leaving home to go to work, watched the horse and cart go tearing past and rushed back into his house.

"A bucket and shovel, quick," he shouted to his bemused wife. "Nutty Slack's hoss...."

"What do you want that at this time of year for, you're not going to do any gardening are you?" she interrupted him.

"Eh?" Tommy looked puzzled for a moment. "Nay yer daft bat, not hoss shit, *coal*, Nutty's hoss is stampeding, there's coal all owert' road. Get a bucket and shovel, quick, before anybody else gets out there. We'll have enough coal to keep t' fire burning for a week!"

Armed with a bucket, a coal scuttle and two shovels they hurried out and began collecting coal from the road, to be joined almost immediately by most of their neighbours, all eager to have their share of this unexpected windfall. All of them ignored the sound of gunfire and the possible danger they were in.

~

Meanwhile, with Nutty frantically pulling at the reins and shouting himself hoarse, Plodder maintained his furious pace for about five minutes, by which time he'd got well away from the confines of the town. He gradually slowed down and stopped, exhausted, trembling and snorting. Furiously, Walter jumped down from his cart; half his load had gone.

"What the hell do you think you're playing at?" Walter

demanded of his horse. Then seeing the look of terror in the animal's eyes, all his anger evaporated. He flung his arms around Plodder's neck and stroked him soothingly.

"It's OK old pal, it's all right, and it's not your fault." He looked about him; they'd left the built-up area of the town and were in the country on the coast road. In the distance he could hear the muffled sound of the gunfire and he could see the smoke hovering like a cloud over the sea and the town, making a dull morning even duller. He couldn't see the warships from here, the jutting cliffs hid the bay, but he knew that an attack from the sea was in progress. He glanced again at his half empty cart, and on the spur of the moment he decided to have a day off. Those of his customers who didn't get a delivery that day would just have to do without; he didn't care any more. Perhaps the time had come for him and Plodder to retire. The horse had calmed down by this time and though still breathing heavily, was standing quietly.

~

" I think we're both getting too old for this, mate. Come on old lad, we'll go and see our Cyril, he lives near here," Nutty said wearily, "And bugger the lot of 'em!" he added vehemently to no-one in particular, as he shook his fist in the general direction of the town. He took the reins and led the horse gently along the road to his brother Cyril's smallholding half a mile away.

8

Georgie Harrison and his friend Raymond Turner, both aged five, waiting their turns to use the outside privy that served the six houses in Oxley's Yard, filled in the time by kicking stones to each other. Occasionally they were a bit too enthusiastic and the stones went higher than they should have done, causing an irate householder to bang on the small front window and threaten them with dire punishment. There were many "Yards" in the lower part of the town, groups of sometimes a dozen or more tiny dark houses, surrounding a small courtyard. They were cramped, overcrowded and lacking in sanitation, having one privy shared by all the families, in each yard; this was cleaned by the women in each family, in strict rotation, several times a week. Oxley's Yard was one of three yards off Quay Street, which ran parallel to Sandside. The children who lived in them had one advantage over children in other parts of town: they had only to cross the road and they had the vast expanse of sands to play on. It was the only advantage.

~

The sound of a rusty bolt being drawn back, followed by the squeak of the latch being lifted, made them pause and get ready to race for the privy as soon as it was vacated. They crouched at the end of the yard ready to run, waiting for crotchety old Daniel Hudson to emerge. This was one of their usual games, whoever lost the race had to go and pinch a penny bullseye from old Mrs Henson's rock shop on the sea front, without getting caught. They would then take turns at sucking the bulls-eye, passing it over each time it changed colour, the one who had won the race in the first place having first suck! They tensed, ready to run, as they saw the privy door slowly open. The old man came out, scowled at the two boys then stamped off to his squalid little house. Ignoring him, the two boys started to run, but Georgie's sister Rosie, older than Georgie by one year, streaked across in front of them and beat them to it. She pulled her tongue out at them as she closed and bolted the door.

"Girls! They always cheat," said Raymond contemptuously, with the expert knowledge of one who had no dealings with the opposite sex. He had no sisters, just four older brothers and two younger ones, all sharing the two up two down cottage with their parents.

"She'll be hours in there," replied Georgie, "she always is. Let's go round to Leslie's." They left Oxley's Yard to find their friend who lived in the next yard down the street. They weren't really desperate for the lavatory and if they were taken short they would just pee in the gutter, as they often did; it was infinitely preferable to using the malodorous privy anyway. As they got to the entrance of the yard, they were able to see the bay and three warships steaming into view. Even as they caught their first glimpse, the ships began to fire, a squawking flock of seagulls flew over their heads and there was an explosion on the Castle just behind them, all in rapid succession. Frightened, the boys turned to run back. Two shells exploded directly in front of them, flinging them both across the yard.

~

It was old Daniel who took charge. He'd seen many horrific injuries during his time at sea, and had learned what to do in an emergency. He saw at a glance that Georgie was already dead. Mercifully Raymond was unconscious, his injuries looked horrendous, his right foot was dreadfully mangled, and almost severed from his ankle. His face and head were covered in so much blood, it was impossible to see how bad the wounds were. The small courtyard was suddenly full as everyone came out to see what had happened. On seeing their sons lying on the ground the mothers of both boys immediately began screaming and wailing, as did most of the other women.

"Take them bloody women inside and give 'em some gin",

was Daniel's first order. A woman was heard to mutter: "Heartless old sod!" but she nevertheless guided Mrs Harrison back into her house murmuring some platitudes of comfort.

~

It wasn't that Daniel was callous, just very insensitive. He was no stranger to tragedy, having lost two sons at sea and a daughter in childbirth. His wife had suffered from tuberculosis for many years and he had watched her fade away gradually, unable to do anything to help her. He didn't want pity from anybody and had created a reputation for himself of being very hard and unfeeling.

"You two," he pointed to two boys, one of whom was Raymond's brother, "you two, shift your bloody arses and run down to Percy Carey's and ask him for a lend of his cart." Percy Carey was a ship's chandler with a shop on Quay Street. He obliged some of his regular customers by delivering their purchases for them on a handcart. Other customers borrowed it to transport items across the road to their boats in the harbour. Percy was always willing to lend his cart - and didn't charge a penny for doing so, although he never refused a gratuity when it was offered, but that didn't happen very often!

~

The boys ran off swiftly. "Get some blankets, and some pieces of cloth," commanded Daniel, to no one in particular; a couple of women quickly went to do his bidding. When one came back with an old smelly blanket and a not too clean sheet, Daniel took the sheet from her and instructed the woman to "Cover that little bugger up," indicating Georgie's broken body. Her husband took the blanket from her and concealed the mangled remains. Daniel ripped part of the sheet into strips, it was thin and threadbare and tore easily. He made a rough tourniquet, then made a pad with the rest of the sheet and held it against what was left of Raymond's foot.

"Here you," he directed a man standing helplessly nearby, "stop gawping and hold this tight." Daniel tied the pad with a strip of cloth. "I doubt it'll do much good. I reckon that foot'll have to come off. Shut up you silly bitch" he added, sharply, as a woman gave a faint scream, "make yersen useful. Get a bowl of water and try cleaning some of this blood off his head, so we can see how bad it is." As she turned to go into her house, the two boys came back with the cart, closely followed by Percy. "Never mind," Daniel called to the woman "wrap this kid up and put him on t' cart. Get him up to t' hospital as quick as you like. But remember, loosen that tourniquet every quarter of an hour or his leg'll drop off!" Several willing hands gently put a blanket round Raymond and carefully lifted him on to the cart. As they did so Daniel cautioned them:

"Mind them bloody bombs, think on, and be as fast as you can. He's lost a lot of blood." With four willing pairs of hands pushing, and two others following, ready to take their turn, they ran up the steep hill towards the hospital. They kept in the middle of the road all the way, dodging debris as it fell off the tall buildings.

Georgie's little body was carried into his parents' wretched narrow house. Old Granny Mallinson, from Drury's yard, was sent for to lay out the tiny corpse. Daniel Hudson stomped back into his dingy cottage and shut the door firmly behind him. He had a reputation for being "a cantankerous old bugger" to maintain; he would have been ashamed if anybody had seen the tears in his eyes. The sight of the pathetic little corpse had affected him more than he could imagine and he didn't give much for Raymond's chances. In spite of his ferocity he was quite fond of the children - but he wouldn't admit it for the world.

9

"Where's our Gordon gone, Mam?" asked nine-year-old Suzanne, at the same time stuffing her mouth with fried bread covered in egg yolk, which ran down her chin in a yellow trickle.

"Don't talk with your mouth full," admonished her sister Laura with the superiority of her eleven years. Connie Harland smiled to herself, as she turned to her two little girls, carefully placing the large frying pan with its sizzling bacon at the side of the cooking range, where it would keep hot without burning. "Yes, Suzie, *don't* talk with your mouth full. I've already told you where Gordon's gone," she said patiently. "Today's the day he's going to have his story in the paper. He's gone to Mr Morley's shop to buy a newspaper. He won't be long. Then he'll show it to you and you can read what it says about him." She turned back to the range, the kettle was boiling, she filled the teapot and left it to stand for a few minutes.

~

Fourteen year old Gordon was a keen Boy Scout, he had been presented with a special award from the District Commissioner, two days before, and an article was to be published today in the local paper. He was so excited about it that he'd rushed off to the shop before breakfast, to buy The Gazette.

He'd never had his name in the paper before. Connie picked up the frying pan again; as she did so an explosion suddenly shook the house, startling her so that she jumped, spilling some fat on the fire. A sheet of flame roared up then almost immediately died down again. Connie instinctively sprang back, but had the presence of mind to replace the pan on the hob.

Suzie screamed, "It's thundering!" She jumped down from her chair and hid under the table. Connie, trying to keep calm and not show her fear, didn't think it was thunder, especially as the loud booms were happening almost continuously. She went into the street, to find that most of her neighbours, many still in their night clothes, had come out to discover what was happening. Rumours were bandied about, the words "Germans" and "Invasion" were repeated more than once. Frank Fletcher, whose father was a fisherman, was just returning from the harbour, where he'd been to find out if his Dad's trawler had come in. He confirmed that he'd seen some ships that he couldn't identify, sailing into the bay. He thought they were German warships, in fact he was almost sure they were. Although the shelling continued, most people decided that there was nothing to be gained by standing in the street, they'd probably be just as secure indoors, and there were breakfasts to be cooked and work to be done. Suzie was still hiding under the table when Connie went back into the kitchen; Laura was trying to coax her out.

"Leave her," said Connie, "if she feels safer there, leave her." She was beginning to be anxious about Gordon. He'd been gone longer than she would have expected, and as the shelling continued she became more worried. She thought up several reasons for his prolonged absence. Maybe he'd had to wait some time in the shop before being served, perhaps he'd met some friends and they were reading the paper, there could be many sound reasons for his prolonged absence. The unexpectedly loud knock at the front door startled her. She hesitated a moment, then with some trepidation opened the door, and found her neighbour Mrs Allison and the local bobby on the doorstep. She vaguely noticed that his cape was full of holes and absently wondered why.

"Connie..." began Mrs Allison, but was interrupted by the constable.

"Mrs Harland, would you come with me please," he said quietly, but with an air of authority that almost made it an order.

"Gordon…" she murmured and went straight out without waiting to don a coat or a shawl.

"I'll stay wit' lasses, don't you worry," called Mrs Allison, but Connie hardly heard her, she'd seen the small group of people at the end of the street and had broken into a run.

~

Gordon was lying on the ground, clutching a newspaper in his hand. Several people tried simultaneously to tell her what had happened, but Connie didn't hear them. She knelt down and took him in her arms. A fragment of shell had hit him. "It's in Mam, look!" He feebly waved the newspaper, opened at the account of the presentation of his award. He smiled at her, and died. For a few seconds Connie didn't realise her son was dead, then she gave a little scream and a wailing cry, she rocked his body in her arms calling his name repeatedly.

10

"I bet I'm the only girl in my class who has to go to Church at eight o'clock on a Wednesday morning," complained Dulcie Morgan as she pulled on her brown kid gloves.

"I bet we're the only girls in the *school* who have to go to Church on a *Wednesday* morning, it's bad enough having to go on Sundays" agreed her sister Charlotte. "We could have another hour in bed! But at least it's not as bad as Mildred Kay's cousin, she has to go *every* morning 'cos she's a Catholic and they have to go every day."

"Gosh!" was Dulcie's incredulous reply.

"Are you girls ready? Do hurry!" came an imperious call from the bottom of the stairs.

"Yes Mother," the sisters demurely chorused in unison, as they went down to the hall where their Mother inspected them. She adjusted Charlotte's hat, which was set at too rakish an angle for a respectable young lady, and pushed Dulcie's hair from her shoulders to hang straight down her back almost to waist length.

"Come along, we'll be late, it's almost eight o'clock." Mrs Morgan led the way out of the house. As they walked along the Esplanade in the morning mist Dulcie looked across the bay.

"Oh look! Ships!" she observed brightly.

"That is *not* unusual Dulcie. Come along, hurry." They crossed the road, turned down the next street and entered the church where the organist was softly playing a voluntary.

Reverend Basil Shaw climbed into the pulpit and scowled at the small congregation. He announced the first hymn, "Onward Christian Soldiers", but as the opening chords of Sullivan's music resounded through the church, the noise of the organ was almost drowned out by a series of loud bangs from outside. The organist and singers faltered for a few seconds but Reverend Shaw did not pause, his deep voice echoed round the building. Taking their lead from him the congregation sang, but with not quite as much confidence as their vicar. As they sat down at the end of the hymn, an exceptionally loud bang like a thunderclap exploded immediately overhead, followed by the sound of falling masonry. Several barely suppressed screams rippled through the church. The verger approached the pulpit with short rapid steps and whispered something to the vicar, who came part way down the pulpit steps to receive the message, then went back to his vantage point. He momentarily surveyed the congregation in silence, then informed them:

"It appears we are being attacked by enemy warships. You are, of course, free to leave if you wish. Personally, I think you will be safer here in God's house than you will be on the streets. He will protect you," the vicar told them confidently. No-one wanted to be the first to move, so everyone stayed where they were, although they weren't all as sure of God's protection as His representative in this church.

"Let us pray," said the Reverend Shaw.

"I knew those ships were Germans, I just knew it," whispered Dulcie to her sister as they knelt down on the scratchy hassocks.

"No you didn't," contradicted Charlotte, "you thought they were ordinary ships"

"Ssh!" hissed Mrs Morgan sharply.

The service proceeded, to the accompaniment of gunfire. After about ten minutes there was a brief lull and the congregation gave an audible sigh of relief, but the interlude was short and soon the shelling re-commenced.

11

"Blast and dammit! Dammit and blast it!" The collar stud that Harold Yeomans, senior Magistrate, Justice of the Peace and respected citizen of the community, was trying to insert into the back of his starched collar slipped from between his finger and thumb and shot across the room.

"Blast and dammit," he repeated as he got down on his knees and crawled along the floor looking for the stud. It was not a very dignified position for a man of his standing so he called impatiently for the maid.

"Elsie!" he shouted. "Elsie! Where is the damn girl?" Harold pulled the bell chord impatiently, he was due in Court in just over an hour, and he hadn't even finished dressing yet. He liked plenty of time to dress, savour his breakfast and peruse the daily papers. He took pride in the fact that he walked to the Court House on the days he had to attend. Admittedly, it took only ten minutes to do so, but he considered it a good form of exercise. Most of his colleagues went by carriage even though they lived no further away than he did.

With a brief knock, the maid came hurrying in, "Yes sir?" she panted breathlessly, having run up two flights of stairs.

"Never mind 'yes sir, no sir,' find my bloody collar stud, it's rolled over there somewhere." He pointed vaguely to a corner of the room. He strode to the window and looked out. The bedroom was at the front of the Georgian terrace house, which was part of an attractive secluded crescent overlooking a central garden, at this time of year seasonally bare, and white with a light covering of frost. In three months' time it would be a colourful panorama of spring flowers, which would be replaced by an equally eye-catching array of summer blooms that would in turn soften to the muted colours of Autumn plants. On the opposite side of the crescent he could see the upper parts of four large detached mansions, secluded and almost hidden by the trees and high walls that surrounded them. They were all owned by the gentry and used mainly as summer residences. During the past few days he had caught glimpses of the two Sitwell boys, from Woodend, the large detached house in the corner. Harold surmised that they must have come for the Christmas holidays, and idly wondered if the rest of the family would be joining them. In the background he had a good view of the sea and the harbour, not as clear today as it might have been, due to the mist. It occurred to him that he had been hearing gunfire for several seconds, but he'd been so het up about the loss of his collar stud, it hadn't penetrated his consciousness. With a sense of shock he saw the vague shapes of warships visible in the mist, the flare of the guns and flames from the direction of the Castle.

"Bloody Huns!" he said incredulously.

Elsie found the stud almost immediately it hadn't gone far. Harold had been looking in the wrong place. Privately she thought it was a lot of palaver about a collar stud, he had plenty more in a box on his dressing table.

"Why on earth didn't he just get another one. Silly old buffer!" she thought. "As if I haven't enough to do without running about after him!" She straightened up. The gunfire made her feel very nervous, and she wanted to get back to the comparative safety of the kitchen below stairs, at the back of the house.

"Here it is, Sir." As Elsie walked forward with the collar stud held out a tremendous explosion shattered the bedroom window. Elsie dropped the collar stud again, she screamed, and went on screaming, as Harold was thrown to the other side of the room. He never received his collar stud, he never knew anything about the shell that killed him.

~

As Judith Yeomans raised the cup of tea to her lips, the whole house shook. She dropped the cup, which smashed to pieces on her breakfast plate and sent a spray of hot liquid all over the front of her clean white blouse. She jumped to her feet, holding her blouse away from her chest. Elsie, on the floor above, screamed and carried on screaming. Judith ran to the bottom of the stairs, arriving there at the same time as Hannah the parlour maid. Quickly they ran to Judith and Harold's bedroom, but stopped abruptly in the doorway, appalled by the scene of devastation. The master was lying in front of the window covered in blood, while Elsie stood in a corner screaming hysterically, she was bleeding profusely from a deep cut in her right cheek. Hannah went over to her and slapped her sharply on the other cheek. Elsie gasped, then began to sob quietly. Hannah pushed the young maid onto a chair and satisfied herself that Elsie's injury was superficial, then turned her attention to her mistress who was cradling her husband's body, her white blouse now stained with blood as well as with tea.

12

Edie Cox hurriedly thrust her three-year-old son's arms into his coat and unceremoniously dropped him into his push-chair, little Martin whimpered at the rough treatment. Edie ignored him as she scribbled a note to her husband and left it on the kitchen table, where he'd find it when he came back from his milk round.

"Where're we going, Mam?" asked her six year old daughter Lucy.

"To Auntie Ellie's. Get a move on, help Reggie do up his coat!" Reggie, at only four and a half, had not yet mastered the art of fastening buttons.

"Why?" came the inevitable question.

"Because he's not big enough to do it himself"

"No! I mean why are we going to Auntie Ellie's?"

"Because she lives further away from the sea and the Germans won't get us there," she said firmly, disregarding the fact that Ellie lived only a five minute walk further away from the sea than Edie did, a distance that was unlikely to deter any invading army.

"Now get a move on," she repeated.

"What will the Germans do to us if they get us?" persisted Lucy.

"They'll take us away and make us into white slaves." Lucy opened her mouth to pursue this interesting topic, but before she could voice her thoughts Edie bundled the children out of the house. She carefully locked the front door and posted the key, which was tied to a piece of string suspended from a nail behind the door, through the letter box. With Reggie and Lucy on either side of Martin's pushchair, she started to walk briskly away, then stopped suddenly.

"Wait there! Don't move!" Edie ordered the three youngsters. They took her command literally and waited, petrified. She ran back into the house and came out within seconds carrying a big brown earthenware tea-pot. She re-locked the door and posted the key again, then she placed the tea-pot on Martin's knee.

"Hold that tightly, don't dare drop it!" Martin put his little arms around the tea-pot and hugged it to him. None of the children dared to ask why they were taking a tea-pot with them to Auntie Ellie's.

13

Brian Hollis was dreaming about soldiers fighting in a war. He could hear the gunfire and men shouting, he dreamt of columns of soldiers marching while shells exploded all around them. The sounds became louder the marching feet came nearer. Brian woke up he could still hear the soldiers marching and the gunfire. He got out of bed and padded across the bedroom floor, the exposed lino icy under his bare feet. He was flabbergasted by what he saw. There were hundreds of people hurrying down the street, well maybe not hundreds, but a lot more than was usual at any time of day. They were all going in the direction of the town centre. With great difficulty he pushed up the sash window.

"Hey mister," he called to a man passing below, "What's up?" The man looked up, and hurried on his way without answering. He tried again, this time he shouted to a woman with a little boy in a pushchair and two other children trotting along on either side. He noticed that the toddler in the pushchair had a teapot on his knee, and wondered why.

"Hey Missus, what's going on?" he shouted. She looked up, "It's t' Germans, they're shelling us from t' sea. They're going to invade us. We're going to me sister's up in Falsgrave." she informed him. "Have you got somewhere to go?" she asked and hurried on without waiting for a reply. Brian felt quite frightened now; he wasn't sure what to do. He was a sensible lad of twelve, but he and his younger brother were in the house on their own. Their mother, a young widow, went out early every morning to scrub some offices, she went straight from that job to a big house on South Cliff where she spent a couple of hours cleaning for a lonely rich old lady called Miss Fox. Every school day, Brian got up about twenty past eight, and woke Donald. The two of them dressed and went downstairs to heat up the porridge their mother had prepared the previous evening, and then they went off to school. She was home to give them their dinner when they returned at midday and was there to give them their tea, when they finished school at the end of the day. At a time when most people were finishing their labours she went out again to clean some more offices for a couple of hours during the evening. Brian and Donald were used to fending for themselves. During the light evenings in Spring and Summer they would play out in the streets with the other children of the neighbourhood. When the darkness came earlier, they would sit together in front of the fire, playing games or reading. Miss Fox had sent them some picture books she and her brothers had used as children and once she had sent them some wooden soldiers.

~

On the morning of the bombardment Brian woke Donald as usual: surprisingly, the child had slept through all the noise. Brian didn't want to alarm his little brother, so he tried to proceed normally. Donald naturally wanted to know what the loud noises were and why there were lots of people in the street. As casually as he could, so as not to worry him, Brian told him what the woman in the street had said, and Donald accepted the information, with the equanimity of a trusting seven year old.

~

"We're not going to school today, we're going to meet Mum from work, and tell her what's happening," Brian told his little brother, successfully hiding his own anxiety. "We might have to go to Grandma's in Leeds, so we'll have to take some clothes with us." He tried to make it sound like an adventure. They didn't possess a suitcase, there'd never been any need for one: people in their situation never went on holiday. Brian found a brown paper carrier bag and stuffed in a few clean clothes that were in the laundry basket waiting to be put away. Donald was very excited, no school and a chance to go and see Grandma in Leeds! He was young enough not to have much awareness of danger; this *was* a big adventure. Brian took the bag in one hand and Donald's hand in the other, the two boys joined the refugees in the street, and went to find their mother at her place of work. Although they didn't know exactly where Miss Fox lived.

14

Stan and Dolly Merriman's general store had already been open for over an hour by the time the bombardment started. The shop had a pleasant appetising smell, a mixture of cured ham, cheese and fresh bread, and other miscellaneous undefined food smells. Early though it was, there had already been several customers, and it would get much busier later in the morning. Dolly was mopping the floor and Stan replenishing the stock on the shelves when Mrs Braithwaite, a regular customer from across the street, bustled in, full of her own importance as usual and bursting to tell them the news about an imminent invasion. Gladys Braithwaite was a large lady, who knew everything, or thought she did. Her information was usually from an unknown source, most of her sentences prefaced with 'they say' although who 'they' were was never divulged. Her source of knowledge on this occasion was from a neighbour who had been told by a friend who had been told by a fisherman who had been on the pier when the warships had sailed into the harbour. She wasn't going to let a few enemy warships disrupt her normal routine - they wouldn't dare!

"Them's Germans, making all that noise, you know, they say they're firing at us from ships ont' sea. I'll have a couple of rashers of that bacon there." She pointed to a side of gammon on a marble slab. "And make sure it's lean, and no gristle. They say there's hundreds of German soldiers waiting to land," she informed them knowledgeably. "You'd best shut up shop and take shelter, or even go away somewhere, they say allt' trains and everything are full with people leaving. I'll not go away," she said virtuously, "there's nowhere to go anyroad. I'll have a dozen eggs, are they fresh? How long have you had 'em in?"

"Freshly laid this very morning Mrs B! still warm from the hens' backsides they are," said Stan cheerfully, as he counted out twelve eggs into the basin Mrs Braithwaite had handed to him.

"There's no need to be coarse," she sniffed. "I don't think they'll invade do you? Anyroad it's all gone quiet, I expect they've gone back to where they came from by now. Have you any Black Pudding? They've sent for t' military you know. Our Norman's going int' army you know, I don't know what for, they say it'll soon be all over." She prattled on, as Stan added up her purchases. The Merrimans, used to Mrs Braithwaite's gossipy hyperbole, listened to only about half of what she said and took the rest with a pinch of salt. Nevertheless, after she had gone, Dolly looked worried.

"Look Stan, I'll just pop up to Mr and Mrs Smith's to see if they're all right, and I'll see if I can find out just what *is* going on. Shouldn't be long." The Smiths were elderly neighbours. Neither was very mobile, and Dolly often called in to see if they were managing, and to take them a few groceries from time to time.

"Right love," said Stan as she left the shop. He opened the trap door and went into the cellar to get some more supplies from its cool depths.

15

"*Ee*-nid, Enid"

"Coming mother," called Enid sweetly, "I've only got one pair of hands, you stupid old witch," she added under her breath. She resented being treated as a maid of all work by her mother. Mrs Mason considered herself to be an invalid; Enid knew she was a hypochondriac, although that wasn't a word in her vocabulary. "She's only putting it on," she told the rest of her family, who thought she was uncaring. "They don't have to put up with her, day in and day out," she told herself time after time. Enid had three married brothers, all younger than she was, who all had supercilious wives and a brood of obnoxious ill-mannered children each. As the only daughter, everyone assumed that Enid would stay at home and look after their mother; that was her duty and vocation. Enid didn't see it that way though, she wanted to be married with a family of her own, but in her position there was no possibility of meeting anyone even remotely suitable, and life was passing her by. She had decided that at thirty-five, she was destined to be an old maid forever. She finished preparing her mother's breakfast tray, as the old lady's querulous voice came again.

"I'm coming, you impatient old bitch, I've only got one pair of hands," Enid said *soto voce.*

"Coming Mother," she called brightly as she climbed the stairs. The bedroom was stuffy, and cluttered with medicine bottles and pillboxes. It smelt of a mixture of medication, stale urine, sweat and lavender water. Even though a fire was blazing in the bedroom grate, Mrs Mason was wearing a thick canary yellow woollen bed-jacket over a red flannel nightgown, and there were several blankets and a heavy quilt on the bed. Enid felt overpowered every time she entered the room. She wanted to fling open the window, dowse the fire and throw away all the bottles of medicines and pills. "That's the first thing I'll do when the old cow passes on," she constantly promised herself, "and it can't come soon enough for me." She smiled pleasantly at her Mother: "Here you are, dear, a nice boiled egg and a slice of bread and butter, with a cup of tea." She put the tray on the bedside table and helped her mother to sit, propped up by pillows.

"It's taken long enough. I hope that egg's not too hard boiled, it was like chewing through a brick yesterday." Mrs Mason always had her breakfast in bed, then sometime during the middle of the morning, she would get up and slowly dress, with Enid's help. Even more slowly she would go downstairs and flop into the large armchair in the front room, where she would spend the rest of the day - "Holding Court" Enid called it - to an assortment of visitors. Family, friends and neighbours all took it for granted that Enid would serve tea and cakes and clear the debris afterwards. She also had three fire grates to clean every day. She had tried to persuade her mother to use the large kitchen instead of the front room to entertain her visitors, but that wasn't good enough. Mrs Mason liked to sit by the big bay window and watch the world go by!

"What's that noise?" asked Mrs Mason, as a series of loud bangs reverberated through the house. She neatly sliced the top off her egg, and peered at the yolk to check if it was the right consistency. Not too runny that it was liquid, and not hard, but somewhere in between so she could dip her toast in it and not have yolk dripping all over the front of her nightdress.

"Is it thunder?"

"Probably, I don't know. What do you fancy for dinner? How about a nice piece of fish?" Enid was anxious to get out of the suffocating atmosphere of the bedroom. "I'll come back later and help you to get dressed."

"No! I don't think it's thunder; it sounds like gunfire to me. I'll come down now. Fetch me dressing gown," she ordered.

There was no point in arguing. Enid removed the breakfast tray from the bed and handed her mother a blue fluffy dressing gown, then helped the old lady downstairs, to the kitchen, whether she liked it or not. There had been no time to light the fire in the front parlour.

16

"Wrap up well, that mist'll get right into your bones, put this muffler on." Audrey Thompkinson handed her husband a thick long hand-knitted woollen scarf, which he wound around his neck, then arranged the ends over his chest, under his overcoat. Geoffrey Thompkinson was preparing to take his regular morning walk along the cliff top with his black and white mongrel dog, Jasper. Geoffrey and Audrey led a very orderly life, quiet and predictable. To outsiders they had a boring existence and were a boring couple. However they were very content living in their little rut, they had been married over thirty years and lived for each other. They had no family; during the early years of their marriage this had been a source of great disappointment, but over the years they had resigned themselves to just being a couple. They were happy in each other's company; they had few friends, and fewer relatives. Audrey had no siblings and Geoffrey's only sister, who had never married, preferring a teaching career, was now headmistress of a large girls' grammar school in Lancashire.

Weather permitting; Geoffrey took Jasper for a walk along the cliff paths just before eight o'clock, each morning. When they reached the cliff top, he'd let Jasper off the lead so that he could run about freely. He strolled along the cliff for ten minutes then went home, collected his brief case and went to work ready to start at half past eight. Geoffrey was the chief accounts clerk at W. Remmington's large department store, a position that suited his meticulous and orderly personality. He had started as office boy when he left school forty years ago and had risen to his present position, which he'd held now for fifteen years. Each evening Geoffrey took Jasper for another walk, again on to the cliff paths, but then turning towards the Spa and the south sands. Every Sunday morning and evening, Geoffrey and Audrey attended church, so they took Jasper for a long walk, during the afternoon instead, after their traditional Sunday roast dinner.. This gave them a good appetite for Sunday tea, which was always cold ham, with homemade bread spread with yellow creamy farmhouse butter, followed by homemade scones, sponge cake, and two cups of tea each. At ten minutes to ten in the evening Geoffrey took Jasper for a final run just around the block. This took exactly ten minutes, and Audrey had a cup of cocoa and a biscuit waiting when they returned. They went to bed at half past ten every night. Jasper knew the routine so well he always went to sit by the front door, tail thumping on the floor, exactly half a minute before Geoffrey came with the lead.

When he noticed the ships sailing into the bay Geoffrey didn't take too much notice at first. He often saw fishing boats and other marine craft entering or leaving the harbour. This was, after all, a fishing port. Geoffrey couldn't identify the ships immediately; their shapes were rather blurred in the surrounding mist. Jasper frisked about, sniffing at the grass, running away from his master then running back, furiously wagging his tail and generally enjoying himself as he did every morning and evening. This was his favourite walk, along the cliffs, he knew he wasn't allowed to go near the edge and instinctively kept a safe distance away, but there was plenty of grass for him to frolic on. He liked to run on the sands too during his evening walk, but he preferred the cliffs. Sometimes Geoffrey would throw sticks for him to retrieve. Geoffrey moved near to the top of the cliff to try and get a closer look at the ships, he stared incredulously as a burst of flame erupted from one of them, followed immediately by gunfire from the others, which continued indiscriminately.

"Goodness gracious! We're being attacked," cried Geoffrey in disbelief, as he realised he was seeing enemy warships: that was the strongest expletive he was ever likely to use. "Come Jasper, let's go," he called to the little dog. Before he had time to turn away a stray shell hit the cliff just below the point at which he was standing. The ground gave way beneath his feet and Geoffrey was catapulted onto the rocks a hundred and thirty feet below. Jasper, running to re-join Geoffrey saw his master disappear and stopped suddenly. He was completely bewildered; he couldn't understand where his master had gone. He was frightened by the loud bangs he could hear and the flashes he could see coming from the direction of the sea. Cautiously he went to the place where he thought he'd last seen his master, but there was only a sheer drop to the sea. He whimpered in perplexity. Jasper, an intelligent dog, knew intuitively that something horrendous had happened and that he was powerless to do anything about it himself. Barking wildly, he frantically ran home, to raise the alarm.

17

Richard Lovell spent many hours at the window of his large house, high on the cliff top, looking through his powerful telescope. Ten years earlier, at the age of thirty two, Richard had had a riding accident: for several weeks afterwards he had been very ill, hovering between life and death. When his condition began to improve he was given the shattering news that he would never walk again: he was paralysed from the waist down. This was a devastating blow to a man in the prime of life, who had always been extremely active, playing tennis and rugby as well as horse-riding. At social events he was also an energetic dancer, the life and soul of the party. His young, fun-loving wife was unable to bear the thought of being tied to a paraplegic, useless to her in every way, and went off with a former beau who still lusted for her even after her marriage to Richard. She took all her jewellery, all her furs and most of her expensive clothes, but she left behind her two young children. Richard had not heard from her since. After Helen had deserted him, Richard's depression increased, he started drinking heavily, he became so bad-tempered, the servants were loath to go near him, and he ignored his children. Fortunately, at only eighteen months and three years old, they were not in a position to understand what had happened, they did not miss their mother because she had paid only infrequent visits to their nursery. They were quite happy and secure with their Nanny.

One day, on one of her regular weekly visits, Richard's sister Louise lost patience with him, and told him in no uncertain manner what she thought of his behaviour.

"Stop wallowing in self-pity," she told him contemptuously, "there are many, *many* people much, *much* worse than you. At least you have plenty of money; *you* don't have to worry about keeping body and soul together. So what if you can't go riding and playing your silly games, do something else. Write a book, read, get a basket chair and get your manservant to take you out!" Louise nagged. "In fact Maynard can learn to drive a motor car and take you on jaunts! Just stop feeling sorry for yourself and start counting your blessings. No wonder Helen left you. Mind you, you're a lot better off without her, flighty young piece that she is, and a rotten mother too!" The tirade went on, with Louise hardly pausing for breath. "Don't deprive your children of a father as well as a mother, Richard!" she concluded earnestly.

Richard was furious with his sister, and ordered her out of the house. She flounced out in a huff, unrepentant and vowing never to set foot over his doorstep again. Nevertheless, Louise's words had struck home and Richard began to pull himself together. It didn't happen overnight, but eventually he began to rearrange his life and come to terms with his disability. He had two large rooms on the ground floor made over for his sole use, one as a living room-cum-study and an adjoining smaller one as his bedroom. The large corner room had wide bay windows in two walls, which gave him panoramic views of the bay. He could see as far as Flamborough Head to the south on clear days. Richard was an early riser and had observed many a sunrise from his window. He breakfasted in his rooms but took all other meals with his children and his secretary. He'd had a powerful telescope installed and spent a lot of time watching the ships entering and leaving the harbour. So powerful was the telescope he was able to read the names on the sides of the ships, and he kept a log of all the sailings. On those nights when he was unable to sleep, and at first there were many, he gazed at the stars. He had taken up his sister's suggestion that he write a book and was now the author of three best sellers. He had very good relationships with his growing son and daughter, Simon and Selina, who had quarters on the first floor with their faithful and much loved nanny. Five years ago when he began writing seriously, Richard had engaged the services of a young woman called Ruth Jenkins to be his secretary. The relationship had gradually grown from employer and employee to friendship and then to love. Richard was now very content; his days were so full he had no time to dwell on his disability.

He never thought about Helen, and he'd long since made up with Louise, who had strongly supported him in his efforts to make a new life, and who approved wholeheartedly of his friendship with Ruth.

Early on this December morning, as Richard was observing through his telescope as usual, he was intrigued to see three strange warships slowly emerge from the mist. He adjusted his telescope, and read the names. Excitedly he rang his bell and called for Ruth.

"Write this down, please, Ruth," he requested her and spelled out the names for her: "*Derrflinger, Von der Tann,* they're German battle cruisers," Richard explained, "and the *Kolberg,* that's a smaller light cruiser." Richard's knowledge of ships had become quite extensive over the last few years. "What are they doing sailing into our harbour? Obviously up to no good." He didn't have long to wait for an answer, the three ships opened fire almost immediately. A movement on the periphery of his vision to the left caught Richard's eye, he swung his telescope round in an arc and caught sight of the man with the little dog that he observed most mornings, on the cliff lower down. He was about to continue his sweep of the bay, when he saw the cliff crumble as some shells hit it lower down. The man fell onto the rocks below. Richard saw the little dog run frantically to the edge of the cliff and back, even from this distance it was possible to see the dog's frenzy, then it swiftly ran away. Richard reached for his telephone, on a table by his side, quickly explaining to Ruth what had happened as he did so. He asked the operator to put him through to the Coastguard, but after a minute or two, was told the line had gone dead. He asked to be put through to the police instead and was soon connected, he reported what he had seen. There was nothing further he could do to help, as the man had disappeared from sight. Richard did not know Geoffrey, but was used to seeing him walking his little dog each morning. He continued to watch the bombardment, Ruth by his side, with her hand on his shoulder, feeling more helpless than usual.

18

As suddenly as it had begun, the shelling stopped. The silence was startling after the continuous noise of the last ten minutes. Smoke hung about in the air, like a black cloud, there was an acrid smell in the atmosphere from the shelling and from several buildings that were on fire.

Iris was still sitting in the cellar with her mother and brother. She didn't like being down there, it was dark and damp, and smelt musty. She worried that there might be mice, or even worse *rats* scratching about. There were only some wooden boxes and a couple of old chairs to sit on; they were too good to throw out completely, but not good enough to have upstairs, and they weren't very comfortable. To try to take her mind off the discomfort inside and the happenings outside, Iris had been thinking about the Church social that she was going to on Saturday. This was going to be a special one as it was also her fourteenth birthday. Last Saturday her mother had bought Iris a new pair of black patent leather shoes with silver buckles, they would look really elegant worn with her red velvet dress with the white lace collar. She dreamed about Edwin Blake: he was three years older than she was, almost grown-up, which meant he would soon feel that he was too old for this kind of event. She liked him a lot and hoped that he would ask her to dance. She liked the socials; there were games and sometimes a Magic Lantern show in addition to the dances. A loud hammering at the door swiftly brought Iris out of her reverie and made them all jump.

"It's t' Germans!" screeched Mrs Appleby, "It's t' Germans!"

"Don't be bloody daft, Ma, Germans wouldn't bother knocking," said Matthew placidly. His mother was so agitated she didn't even chastise him for swearing, or for calling her daft. Matthew was correct, it wasn't the Germans hammering on the front door; it was Joey Holton, one of five fishermen brothers who lived next door.

"Are you all right, Missis? They haven't gone yet, but they've stopped shelling - for now at any rate. You'll be safer across t' road under t' wharf. Come on, I'll take you over. Everybody else is going. Me mam's there already," Joey told them.

"I'll go and see if Gran's all right first," said Matthew.

"Be careful, son," cautioned his mother as he went off up

the hill to where his grandmother lived. Iris grabbed her coat from a hook on the wall and hastily put it on over her nightie; she saw her new shoes under the chair, and snatched them up as her mother hurried her out of the house. They ran quickly across the road with Joey to shelter under the pier.

They were shocked by the devastation they saw along the sea front. Several buildings were burning, there were flames coming from the Castle headland, the Grand Hotel looked as if it had lost all its windows. They heard the clanging bells from several fire engines; the emergency services had never had a disaster of such proportions before, but they were rising to the occasion magnificently.

"A little lad's been killed over yonder," Joey indicated a point further along the sea front, "and his mate had half his foot blown off."

"Who was it? Anybody we know?" asked Mrs Appleby.

"Aye, little Georgie Harrison was killed and Raymond Turner was badly injured."

Iris gasped with horror. She knew the two boys, they were both only five years old.

~

"Are you OK, Gran?" Matthew burst in on his Grandmother and found the old lady calmly blackleading her kitchen range, as she did every morning - except, of course, the Sabbath.

" 'Course I'm all right. Why shouldn't I be?" she demanded sharply.

"Well we're being bombarded from the sea, by some German warships," explained Matthew.

"Bombarded? You mean it's only gunfire? Thank the Lord for that; I thought it was thunder. I don't like thunder," she added as she calmly carried on with her blackleading. Matthew laughed at her composure.

"Don't you think you'd be safer coming back with me? They're all under t' pier. You could be killed in here."

"I'm not going under no pier, to freeze to death. If the Lord wants me to be killed I'll be killed whatever. Anyroad it's stopped now." Her tone of voice indicated that there was no disputing this, and Matthew wouldn't dare argue with her.

"You get back to your Mother, she'll be worrying about you. She always did worry about nowt did our Ida." There was no point in protesting; once Gran had decided something there was no moving her, so Matthew reluctantly turned to leave. Before he reached the door, the bombardment had started again.

"I reckon you'd best stay here," said his Grandmother. "Light t' fire and put t' kettle on while I side these away." She gathered up her cleaning materials and put them in their place in the bottom of the cupboard, then washed her hands at the yellow stone sink, in cold water from the solitary tap. Matthew soon had a pot of tea ready. Secretly he was pleased to be staying, he didn't fancy the prospect of standing in wet sand in the cold misty morning, even though he was concerned about his mother and sister, and he certainly didn't like the idea of being exposed to the German shells. His Gran was quite right: he would probably be safer here than outside. He told himself that in spite of her brave words his Gran needed him, and this was justification enough to stay with her.

19

A few casualties had already come into the Hospital; most were minor injuries, caused by flying glass, others were more serious. Matron, Miss Alice Richardson, was a formidable lady and a dedicated nurse. She had started her nursing career thirty-five years earlier when she was eighteen, very much against the wishes of her upper middle class family. They didn't see any need for her to work at all, but neither the life of a social butterfly nor that of a wife and mother attracted her. She would not be swayed from her purpose in life. Her family accepted her resolve, ungraciously, but were consoled by the thought that it would only be temporary and Alice would soon marry and give up all that nonsense. She had proved them wrong, and paradoxically they were now very proud of her achievement.

It was a hard life for a young probationer, there didn't seem to be much actual nursing to begin with, and all her time seemed to be spent scrubbing floors, washing bedpans, and sterilising instruments. The only time she was allowed near patients in those days was to give them bed baths and rub pressure points. However, she had a true vocation and none of the hardships she encountered deterred her from her chosen profession. She was an ardent admirer of Florence Nightingale and her devoted band of nurses. Alice Richardson was a veteran of the Boer war: she had been one of the first nurses to volunteer for service in South Africa and had nursed both Boer and British wounded impartially, under harsh conditions in the Transvaal. Over the years, she had worked in large hospitals in affluent areas, in small hospitals in poverty stricken areas, where there were few facilities or comforts, and she had also taken on occasional private nursing for society ladies - she wasn't too keen on the latter. In her opinion it was not real nursing. She had taken over as Matron of the Friarage Hospital a few months ago, thinking the time had come to have a quieter and more settled life than she'd had in the past. A quiet seaside town was just what she wanted.

Matron Richardson expected the same devotion to duty from all her staff, as she gave herself. She was very strict in the running of her hospital, but she was very fair, and was respected by all her staff. Liked by most of them, she was even held in affection by a few, a fact that would have surprised her had she known. Unlike some people who had reached the top of their professions, Miss Richardson had not forgotten what life was like at the bottom of the ladder, and was sympathetic to the plight of young trainees; although she would rather die than let them know it!

Matron Richardson summoned the four ward sisters to her office:

"I've spoken to the Coastguards and to the Police," she announced without preamble. "Mr Philips from the coastguard station has just been in to see me and so has Sergeant Jarvis. They have advised me that this is likely to turn into a major disaster, as we'd already suspected. It is going to stretch our resources to the absolute limits. Firstly, I want you to see how many patients on each of your wards may be healthily discharged immediately: we need all the available beds for the worst of the potential casualties. Secondly, contact as many off-duty nurses as possible - we'll need all the help we can use. I know I can rely on you. That is all ladies, thank you!" She dismissed them.

20

Further up the town, at the Railway Station, Freddie Atkinson, the booking clerk, opened the shutters at the ticket desk in response to violent knockings. Usually at this time of day there were only a few businessmen travelling to York or Leeds, many of whom had season tickets and therefore did not need to visit the booking office. He was taken aback by the number of impatient, agitated people in a disorderly queue. There was a lot of pushing and shoving. The first man at the window thrust a handful of coins at Freddie.

"A single!" he said, abruptly. "Where to?" asked Freddie. "Anywhere, anywhere!" was the testy reply. Freddie gave him a ticket to York, and he ran through the barrier to board the train that was standing at the platform. Single handedly, Freddie sold tickets to a legion of people for destinations all over the country. It was not usually necessary to have more than one booking clerk on duty at this time of day. Freddie couldn't recall a time when there had been so many people, but then the town had not been bombarded before. Some passengers, like the first, didn't know where they wanted to go and accepted whatever they were given. The ticket inspector, a burly middle-aged man called Billy Bowman, a veteran of the Boer war, was overwhelmed by the numbers wanting to board the train and unwittingly let many through the barrier without tickets. He was bemused by the state of dress, or rather undress, of some of the people passing through. One man wearing a top hat and frock coat, had apparently forgotten his trousers in his haste, and a middle-aged lady was wearing a white flannelette nightgown under her coat and had only bedroom slippers on her feet. Some people carried lots of luggage; others had none. Neither he nor Freddie placed any credence on the explanation for such an exodus: that the Germans were invading and had already landed on the beach. Most of the refugees were panicking and hysterical, and Billy felt contemptuous that able bodied men could flee from a situation that probably wouldn't arise. Even if it did they should stay and defend their homes and families. He had more sympathy with the women and children; they were not expected to deal with a war situation.

The first train on its way to York pulled out filled to capacity. Those left on the platform ran to another, where the train to Hull was due out shortly. That, too, soon filled up. As each train arrived in, it was soon loaded beyond safety levels. Destinations printed on tickets were ignored: as long as they were getting away from the bombardment and threat of invasion few people seemed to care where they were heading.

21

Connie sat staring into space clutching the newspaper she'd taken from Gordon's dead hands. Someone, she didn't know who, had taken Laura and Suzie away somewhere. The two little girls had been frightened and subdued, not sure of what had happened. Connie's husband, Jim, had been sent for, and was at this moment on his way home from the printing works. PC Hardcastle had brought Connie back to the house, and left her with kindly Mrs Allison who was now trying to persuade her to drink some tea, but Connie paid no heed, showing no awareness of her surroundings. Gordon's body had been brought back to the house by two neighbours, under the supervision of PC Hardcastle, and was now lying on the narrow bed in his little room, awaiting the services of Mrs Hennessy who, in her own words, made her living by "bringing 'em into this world and making 'em look presentable for t' next."

Jim burst in, white-faced and disbelieving, jolted by the news that had been broken to him at work. He took Connie in his arms, she burst into tears and sobbed uncontrollably. Jim held her tightly as he, too, began to weep.

22

"Morning, Mrs Ellis," called Stella Reynolds as she entered the warm kitchen after a brief knock at the door. "By heck, something smells good." Mrs Ellis had already started her baking, and the air was filled with the appetising aroma of fresh scones. A bowl of bread dough giving off an inviting yeasty aroma stood in the hearth covered by a clean white floured cloth. By the time the Ellis family had finished their day's work there would be fresh crusty bread ready for them. Stella, and Anne Ellis, were both employed at the new Co-operative department store. Stella called for her friend every morning, and they walked to work together.

"I didn't think you'd be coming today Stella, I don't like the sound of that gunfire. I'm not sure that it's safe for you to go out in this," said Mrs Ellis, as her daughter entered the room, with her coat on and in the process of adjusting her hat.

"In what?" asked Anne.

"Well, all this bombing of course," was the impatient reply.

"We'll be all right; anyway it's stopped now."

"We'll be all right, Mrs Ellis," echoed Stella, "anyway it's all down on t' sea front, they won't get us here."

"Well ... I don't know." Mrs Ellis was uncertain, but Anne had decided.

"We'll be late, we can't afford to have our wages docked. Come on Stella. 'Bye Mum, don't worry, it's all over now."

"'Bye Mrs Ellis," called Stella, cheerily. "Only three more days eh?"

"Yes, Stella, only three more days," said Mrs Ellis patiently. "As if I didn't know!" she added under her breath, with a mixture of amusement and impatience. Every day for the last few weeks she'd had a countdown to Anne's wedding day which was to be on Saturday, now, as Stella had pointed out, only three days away.

The girls had been friends all their lives, they lived a couple of doors from each other; they were the same age and had been all through school together. They were exact opposites. Although Stella was the elder by two months, people often assumed that Anne was a few years older than her friend. Anne was a quiet serious girl, rather shy with people she didn't know. Stella had a bubbly personality and hardly ever stopped talking; in fact, according to her mother she was born talking and even talked in her sleep! Stella's red-gold, curly hair, turned-up nose and freckled face, while attractive to others were a torment to her. She longed for silky long black hair, a smooth pale complexion and a straight nose - just like Anne actually.

~

Both girls enjoyed their work in the Co-op building, opened only a few months ago and housing in addition to several departments a bank and offices. Anne was a salesgirl in the Ladies' dress department on the first floor; her pleasant manner and genuine interest in her customers were well suited for this position. She was very sincere and would not try to sell a garment that did not suit a particular lady, but would offer suggestions, which were invariably reliable. Anne knew at a glance what would look flattering and advantageous to her customers, and as they got to know her, the regulars sought her advice.

Stella worked in haberdashery on the ground floor. She adored working in that department and she delighted in telling anyone who would listen where she worked. She loved the sound of the word "haberdashery." She often practised saying it, putting emphasis on different syllables - *hab*erdashery, haber*dash*ery, haber*dash*ery - she couldn't decide which pronunciation she preferred, so she used each of them in turn. She enjoyed arranging and re-arranging the buttons, bows, ribbons and laces in the display cases and on the counter. The regular customers liked being served by her, because she was always cheerful and helpful. She had an eye for colour and design and knew which buttons or ribbons would look well with each fabric. Sometimes her ideas seemed rather outlandish, but when the amateur dressmakers tried out her suggestions they found the finished products had an originality that drew compliments.

The store had been especially busy during the last few weeks, with customers buying Christmas gifts, party frocks and accessories for the festive season. The shop was festooned with colourful decorations, and staff and customers alike had an air of gaiety and suppressed excitement as the holiday approached. Christmas Day was on a Friday this year and the manager had decided that the shop would remain closed on Boxing Day also: he didn't expect much business that day anyway, so they would have a whole three days away from work. The break would be very welcome after the hectic pre-Christmas rush.

As the girls walked to work Anne let Stella ramble on. As usual, as it had been for the last few weeks, her theme was the forthcoming wedding. Anne's fiancé, John Somerford, was a regular soldier, a sergeant in the King's Own Yorkshire Light Infantry - the Koylis. They hadn't seen each other for nearly three years, because John had been stationed in India, so their courtship had been maintained by letters, however neither had any doubts about marrying so soon after the long separation. All the wedding preparations had been left to John's mother, his future mother-in-law and his fiancée. The three ladies had worked well together, Mrs Somerford had arranged the church and the venue for the wedding breakfast, Mrs Ellis had made and lavishly decorated the wedding cake and was to do most of the catering, with help from her sister. Anne with help from her mother and Stella, had made her own wedding dress. It was white satin with a full skirt, the bodice was covered in lace, the long sleeves were decorated with small pearl buttons at the cuffs, and the neckline was decorated with tiny satin roses, each with a seed pearl at its centre. Stella was to be bridesmaid, and the two girls had together made her leaf-green dress that contrasted well with Stella's hair, and made her look quite stunning.

John's regiment had recently been posted back to England to help in the current conflict, and John had ten days leave starting from ...

"Today," declared Stella, "John will be home for tea, aren't you absolutely thrilled? Gosh, he'll be eating your Mum's lovely new bread and scones, the thought of them's making me feel hungry and it's not long since I had breakfast. How on earth are you going to get through the morning? I wish it was Saturday now, don't you?" Anne let her babble on, nodding and smiling from time to time to indicate she was listening. She was quite used to Stella, having put up with her chatter most of her life - well, as far back as she could remember.

"Well, at least you'll be able to go and meet him." Today, being Wednesday was early closing day and the girls would be free from one o'clock. John's train was due in at three o'clock.

"And you'll have the whole of Christmas together... Oh God!" Stella interrupted herself, "That bombing's started again, but I expect we'll be all right here, we're far enough away from the harbour."

"I expect so," replied Anne, "but let's hurry up and get inside anyway." As they ran across the road to the Co-op a volley of shells hit the corner of the building, and a hailstorm of glass and masonry fell on the girls before they could reach the safety of the doorway, burying them under a pile of debris.

23

Casualties were coming in thick and fast to the hospital. There was a grave shortage of beds for those who needed to be admitted. Many off-duty staff had come in voluntarily, but many more were still needed. Several patients had volunteered to be discharged to free their bed for the newcomers. In the women's surgical ward Sister Fenton was having a battle of wills with Mrs Stafford, who had insisted on going home even though she was still recovering from a major operation.

"I promise, Sister, I'll just sit around and let the family wait on me, I won't be doing any more at home than I am here," was Mrs Stafford's unconvincing argument as she looked Sister Fenton straight in the eye. Diana Fenton sighed, Dora Stafford meant what she said, but it was inevitable that in a short time she'd be admitted again, her recovery retarded by slaving for her large family and indolent drunkard husband. However, Dora was a redoubtable lady and as Diana had other patients to think about, she gave in:

"All right, Mrs Stafford, get your things. But please remember you have had a serious operation and you are not as well as you think you are. You must rest as much as possible and call the doctor if you feel ill and … "

"Yes, yes, Sister, I know, I know!" Dora interrupted, and went off to gather up her possessions. With another deep sigh Diana hastened away to see to the new patients that were now coming in a steady stream.

A similar scene was being re-enacted in the men's medical ward. Adrian Conroy was a young doctor newly qualified, and he was no match for Jack Watson, a tough old ex-fisherman.

"Give me one good reason why I should stay here and take up a bed when there's them that'll need it more than me?" he challenged.

"Well, Mr Watson, you're not a well man, you need to stay

here for care and treatment," said Dr Conroy earnestly. "What else can you do for me? You know there's no hope for me - is there? I may as well go home to die rather than die in here," Jack replied belligerently. "I'd rather die at home anyway," he added quietly, with resigned acceptance.

"Now, now Mr Watson, don't talk like that, where there's life there's hope you know," Dr Conroy said encouragingly, but the trite platitude didn't sound very convincing even to himself. Jack laughed mirthlessly:

"Who are you kidding, mate? Tell the truth, lad - there's *no* hope, I've known that for a long time." Adrian Conroy admitted defeat. "All right, Mr Watson, I'll discharge you. I - er I'm sorry," he added sincerely, but inadequately.

"Not your fault lad, I'll be off as soon as I've got me stuff together," was the brisk reply. They shook hands and the young doctor, sad that he was unable to help Jack, but knowing it was no use arguing, went to see what he could do for the bombardment casualties.

Matron Richardson was personally supervising the new admissions.

"Goodness gracious, what's this?" she exclaimed, as behind her she heard Sally Foster giggle.

"That will do, nurse!" she said sharply, even though she felt like giggling herself. Two nuns, their large white wimples flapping like wings at the side of their foreheads, were gliding down the corridor; that was the only way to describe the way they moved - gliding.

"I wonder if they've got wheels on their feet," thought Sally as she stifled another giggle.

"I am Sister Cecilia and this is Sister Frances. Mother Superior has sent us to help, we're both trained nurses," said the elder of the two without prelude. "Where do you want us to start?"

Matron was dumbstruck. "Er, well, yes thank you. Would

you like to see to the injured as they're brought into casualty?" she went on more confidently. "Thank you, we're very grateful for your help." Sister Cecilia nodded graciously and without wasting any more time the nuns rolled up their sleeves, donned large white pinafores over their habits and set to work treating and comforting the injured.

24

Ted Cox was popular with his customers, always courteous and helpful. Like Albert Bell the postman, Ted didn't see any reason to abandon his milk round, just because a "bunch of Huns" was trying to intimidate innocent people. That was how he saw it anyway and he wasn't alone with that philosophy: all the postmen, milkmen and delivery men carried on their morning rounds as usual, in defiance of the attackers.

"Morning, Mrs Johnson," Ted greeted his first customer with his usual cheeriness, "and how are you today?"

"Fair to middling, tha' knows," was Mrs Johnson's stock reply. "I wasn't sure you'd be coming this morning, what with all that shelling like."

"Now would I let you down, Mrs Johnson?" Ted measured out her pint of milk and carried on from door to door with a cheerful word for each customer. His horse Barney patiently followed him up the street, he knew the round as well as Ted did and he was a favourite with all the customers, especially the children who fed him sugar lumps.

A sudden boom startled everyone: the shelling had started again. Ted gasped in horror as he saw Barney fall over, pulling the milk cart with him. "Barney?" he whispered, then louder "Barney!" Several people rushed to the horse, Ted was there ahead of them, but there was nothing to be done. Barney had a large hole in his side and was dead before he hit the ground.

"Oh Barney," sobbed Ted as he knelt by the horse's head. "Barney."

Devastated, and oblivious of any danger they might be in, Ted's customers stood in shocked silence, not knowing what to do, many with tears streaming down their faces, as the milk, mingling with Barney's blood, flowed down the gutter in a pink stream.

Mrs Johnson came up behind Ted and put her arms around his shoulders.

"Don't take on so, lad, he was an old 'un and he'd had a good life," she tried to comfort him.

"Think on - it could have been a bairn." Ted knew she was talking sense but it was too soon to find any comfort in the truth. Barney had been a good reliable horse and Ted was very fond of him. His sudden death was the loss of a great friend.

"Come on in and have a cup of tea lad," invited Mrs Johnson, "it's good for shock and you've had a shock. Well, we all have," she added. Ted allowed himself to be led away, leaving Barney and the milk cart where they'd fallen. A neighbour called to them:

"Taylor's lad has gone to t' post office, Ted, they'll telephone the dairy and let 'em know what's happened." Ted nodded dumbly, and raised his hand in a half salute. There was a small sub-post office at the bottom of the hill, a message would soon be passed to the dairy and arrangements made to remove Barney's body.

25

Brian and Donald had reached the toll bridge that spanned the valley eighty feet below, uniting the main part of the town with the South Cliff area, and obviating the necessity of descending into the valley and climbing the steep hill on the other side - but only if one had the necessary toll fee. Brian and Donald hadn't any money at all.

"It's a penny each, I've told thee, and if tha' can't pay tha' can't cross," said the official in the tollbooth with a finality that defied argument.

"We have to find our Mother," explained Brian, "she works over t' bridge."

"I can't help that. Ye'll have to go down into t' valley and go up t'other side." The man was unsympathetic. "It'll be safer that way anyroad, ye'll get yer head blown off if tha' goes across there, ain't you heard them bombs?" He turned and retreated to the far corner of his booth, picked up the newspaper he'd been reading before the boys came, and took no further notice of them.

It was a waste of time arguing with officialdom, so taking Donald's hand again, Brian guided him down the road called Plantation Hill, into the valley. As they walked towards Ramshill, which would take them up to the South Cliff, they could see the lighthouse with the Castle in the background, framed in the span of the Spa bridge. As they got nearer they caught their first glimpse of the warships, silently menacing at anchor in the bay.

"Hey up, you young devils, where're you off to?" the voice of Andy Nelson startled them. Andy was fifteen and had been working as a delivery boy for a town centre grocer, for just over a year. One of his duties each day was to push a handcart full of orders for delivery to the grocer's wealthier customers who lived on the South Cliff. Brian and Donald knew him quite well; he lived in the same street as they did.

"We're off to find me mum, a lady told us the Germans are invading and we should get away, the man on the bridge wouldn't let us cross because we didn't have no money and … "

"Hold on, hold on," Andy stopped Brian's outpourings. "That bloody bridge wasn't built for the likes of us, tha' knows. That old skinflint that I work for won't pay a penny for me to take these fancy goodies to his snooty customers, who can't be bothered to do their own shopping - the miserable old bugger! So I've to bring this bloody cart all the way down one hill then up that other bloody hill," he complained. He indicated the wooden handcart with its metal wheels, the contents protected by a tarpaulin. "Well, it brings itself down t' hill," he continued. "I have to hang on to stop the bloody thing running away. I could do with a team of hosses to pull it up t'other side. But you shouldn't have come down here today; it's too bloody dangerous. They might start firing again at any minute. The buggers haven't gone yet. You could get yer head blown off!" he added, reiterating the warning made by the tollbooth keeper. "Come on while t' going's good, grab hold!" he invited them. Donald and Brian each took hold of a handle of the cart and helped Andy to push as they crossed the road by the Aquarium - the glass domed building housing an underground entertainment complex and indoor swimming pool.

Ben, Maurice and Colin decided that this might be a good time to leave their vantage point behind the Spa wall. They feared the shelling might start again, as the ships showed no sign of leaving. They caught up with Andy, Brian and Donald as they reached the Aquarium, just as the bombardment started again. None of them could explain later exactly what happened next: they saw a flash like lightening from the tram wires just as a tram started its climb up Vernon Road, then they saw it come hurtling backwards down the hill, completely out of control. "Run!" shouted Maurice, he seized Donald's hand and started to charge up Ramshill, closely followed by Ben with Brian. Andy let go of his cart as he and Colin came up behind in hot pursuit. When they were what they judged to be a safe distance from the runaway tram, and also sheltered from any stray shells from the sea, they turned and watched. They saw a man pick himself up from the road at the bottom of Vernon Road; they assumed he was the conductor. The driver was clinging to the steering wheel, there was nothing he could do to stop the momentum. The tram reduced Andy's cart to rubble, smashing it and its contents into fragments, before crashing through the wall surrounding the Aquarium and coming to rest in the dome, where it hung precariously. Cautioning Donald and Brian to stay where they were the other young men, and the tram's conductor, went to the aid of the driver, helping him to climb out of the rear door of the tram. It was an extremely hazardous operation with the bombardment from the sea continuing, and the tram almost vertical, with one end actually inside the Aquarium, but they managed it eventually. Surprisingly, the driver, although dazed and shaken, did not appear to be injured, fortunately there were no passengers in the tram, and there was nobody inside the Aquarium. He sank down on the ground and assured his rescuers that he was uninjured and would be fine, once he got his breath back. Satisfied that the driver was indeed all right, the young men turned to continue on their way.

"*Jee-zus!*" Andy cried out, "just look at my bloody cart. What am I going to tell the old bugger? He'll kill me!"

"Not your fault, lad," comforted Maurice, "We'll come with you later and explain to your boss what happened, he'll understand, I'm sure. Now let's get out of this." Andy wasn't convinced; his boss wasn't the understanding sort, but he followed the others as they sped up Ramshill, first ensuring that the tram driver and his mate did not need any further aid, to find Miss Fox's house and reunite Brian and Donald with their mother. The upended tram was firmly wedged in the roof of the empty aquarium, but was not a danger to anyone. The tram driver and conductor sat on the ground for a few more minutes trying to recover from the shock, then they made their way shakily up Vernon Road, back to the depot to report what had happened. Halfway up the hill the driver suddenly bent double and was violently sick in the gutter.

26

Edie knocked on the door of her sister's house with her left hand, as she simultaneously opened it with her right. She ushered Lucy and Reggie inside, took the teapot from Martin, freed him from his pushchair and left it at the bottom of the stairs, where it was in everybody's way.

Joshua and Janet were sitting at a square wooden table that took up most of the centre floor space, eating porridge. They grinned at their cousins as they crowded in. Ellie came in from the scullery. "Aye, I thought you might come," she said without surprise. "Is Ted at work? Joss shouldn't be long; his shift finishes at eight. He should be here any minute." Ellie's husband, Joss Armstrong, was a baker who worked nights. "Put that bloody carriage in t' front room, you can't get past it there. What on earth have you brought that teapot for? Did you think I hadn't got one of me own? It's me mother's isn't it?" As she grumbled on she seated her niece and nephews at the table with their cousins, gave them each a slice of bread and dripping, then poured out a cup of strong tea for herself and her sister.

Edie took the pushchair into the rarely used front parlour,

which was decidedly chilly and smelt musty. She rejoined her family and sat down in a shabby comfortable armchair at the side of the fireplace, with the cup of tea in her hand, while Ellie continued her interrogation. "Is there a lot of damage? Is t' town flattened? Mr Simmons next door thinks t' Germans are going to invade. Did you see any?" When she paused for breath, Edie tried to answer some of her, mainly, rhetorical questions.

"I keep all me tanners in t' tea pot, there must be nearly five pounds worth in there now. It's for Christmas. I think most of t' damage is down on t' sea front. No, I didn't see any Germans. I think they're on t' ships out at sea. I think they've stopped now, I've heard nowt for a few minutes." Even as she spoke, there was an almighty explosion that shook the house and rattled the crockery on the table; this was followed by several more, all seemingly quite close at hand.

"They've started again," said Ellie unnecessarily, "What shall we do?" For the first time she seemed a bit uncertain.

"I expect we'll be as safe here as anywhere. I've left a note for Ted, so's he'll know where we are. Here, you bairns, get under t' table and play," Edie ordered. All the children scrambled under the table and sat there, giggling. "It's a solid table. If t' roof falls in it'll give 'em some protection.," she said hopefully. She and Ellie, outwardly calm, continued drinking their tea, and waited for whatever was to come.

27

"I really think you would be safer in Mr and Mrs Brayshaw's cellar, my dear." Herbert Wedderburn took off his spectacles and polished them, as he gazed earnestly at his wife. There was a mark on each side of his nose, like fingerprints, where his *pince nez* had pressed into the skin. He replaced them, pushing them in place with his index finger.

"But we hardly know them, Herbert, whatever will they think?" replied his wife, Emily plaintively. "I'd rather stay with you." She had the cowed nervous air of a woman completely in awe of her husband. She always acquiesced in everything he expected of her without question, including the sex act to which she submitted unwillingly every Friday night. She looked forward to Fridays with some trepidation and revulsion, and was always extremely relieved when the embarrassing, distasteful process was over for another week. She suspected that he had a mistress, maybe more than one. This did not disturb her, in fact she was quite glad, it meant that he did not bother her as much as he used to. When they were first married, she sometimes had to endure his unwelcome advances several times a week and on some occasions more than once during the night. How Emily had hated it.

"Oh, they won't mind," Herbert said heartily, once more taking off his spectacles, polishing them with his handkerchief and replacing them. "You can't come with me, I have to go and open the shop. I'll be needed, I'll be inundated," he said happily, "everybody'll need bandages and ointments for their injuries and pills for their nerves." Herbert Wedderburn owned a chemist's shop. Devastating though the bombardment might be - it would be good for trade! Well, for his trade at least.

"Come along, Emily," he urged, "come along, girls," he said to his two pale-faced daughters: aged ten and seven years they were younger copies of their pale-faced mother. Obediently they followed him out of the house, to a neighbour three doors down the street. Herbert knocked loudly on the door, and elderly Mr Brayshaw opened it within a few minutes.

"Ah, good morning, Sir," said Herbert pleasantly, polishing his spectacles yet again. "I know you won't mind my wife and daughters sheltering in your cellar during this bombardment, I don't like leaving them in the house alone. I must go and open my shop. I'll be needed, you know, I'll be needed. I know they'll be safe with you. Thank you so much." Without giving time for a reply, Herbert raised his hat, lightly kissed his wife on the cheek and quickly walked away. Taken aback, Mr Brayshaw had no choice but to invite his unexpected guests into the house, or otherwise close the door in their faces and leave them standing on the doorstep! He was too much of a gentleman to do that.

Instead of going straight to his shop, Herbert turned in the opposite direction to a terraced house two streets away. The door was opened before he'd finished knocking, by a blonde young woman wearing a pink satin peignoir, trimmed with white fur. She'd obviously been looking out for him.

"Oh Bertie! I've been hoping you'd come. I was quite frightened," she cried as she flung her arms around him and clung to him.

"Don't worry, Irene my love, you'll be quite safe," Herbert comforted his mistress, "I'm here now. Anyway, I do believe it has ceased," he said pontifically, as he disentangled himself from her embrace, then he added hastily: "But I can't stay too long. I must open the shop. I'll be needed, there are bound to be injured people requiring the services of a chemist."

As he was speaking Herbert ushered Irene inside the house, looked up and down the street to see if he was observed by the neighbours, then shut the door. The room was untidy but warm, the fire had been banked up overnight. Irene used the poker to stir it into life and put a couple of medium-sized pieces of coal on. Herbert agitatedly polished his spectacles again. "I really must go, my dear, I'll be needed you know. There'll be people injured, they'll need medical supplies," he said again, happy at the thought of booming business.

"Well, you can stay a while, can't you?" Irene pleaded, "*I* need you! I didn't know what was happening, I've been all on edge. Anyway, they can go to t' hospital or to a doctor."

"Yes, yes, but I need to open the shop. I must go, really I must, I only came to see if you were all right." Irene came close to him, put her arms around his neck and put her cheek next to his. He could smell her perfume, he was instantly aroused, as she knew he would be, she also knew that he would be staying. She started helping him off with his coat. Herbert protested weakly, "I really must go, you know," but did nothing to stop her. He tried to take off his glasses to polish them again, but Irene's embrace was too restricting.

The barrage began again, this time the gunfire seemed nearer.

"We'll stay down here in front of the fire where it's warm," Irene whispered. "This'll be the most exciting one yet, making love on the hearth rug to the sound of gunfire!" She made it sound almost romantic. "I don't feel frightened now that you're here." Herbert had no resistance left. "Well, perhaps just a few minutes, then I really must go." As Irene pulled him down on to the floor, the house collapsed on top of them.

28

In the house next door, Enid Mason had just assisted her mother downstairs. With a large shawl wrapped around her shoulders and a woollen rug over her knees, she was now comfortably seated in the rocking chair in the kitchen/living room, sipping tea from a china cup. This room, like the bedroom, was also cluttered, but instead of the range of medicine bottles, the whole mantelpiece was taken up with brass ornaments. There was more brass hanging on the walls, vying for space with family photographs. The fireplace, surrounded by a large brass fender, had a brass companion set in one corner. It was all shining and well polished - Enid spent hours cleaning it every Friday morning. She hated it; that was another thing that was going to go when her mother passed on. Enid was in the scullery filling the kettle to heat some water to wash up the breakfast pots, when without warning the ceiling came down on her head. She just had time to shout "Mother!" then everything went black.

29

Dolly Merriman was hurrying back to the shop, after ensuring her elderly neighbours were in no immediate danger. They had assured her they were not worried and were very philosophical, Mr Smith merely informing her calmly and politely that:

"If we get killed, we get killed and there's nowt anybody can do about it! Anyroad we'll die together," he'd added, with unarguable logic. He had, however, been grateful for Dolly's thoughtfulness in coming to see how the elderly couple were faring, and thanked her accordingly. "She's a grand lass is Dolly," said Mr Smith as he closed the door. "She is that," agreed his wife.

The shelling began again when Dolly was a mere hundred yards from the shop. She saw the front window of the shop cave in as a shell went through it. "Oh my God, Stan!" She began to run, she didn't know what had hit her, or even that she had been hit, until she found herself on the ground feeling an agonising pain in her shoulder and with blood streaming from a gash in her head. The street was fairly quiet, not many people having ventured out during the onslaught, but Henry Pike on his way to work at the fish filleting sheds saw

Dolly fall and rushed to her aid. She was conscious and moaning faintly. He thought he heard her say "Stand."

"Nay lass, don't try to stand up, just hang on, I'll get help." Fortunately, a hansom cab was coming down the hill towards them. To make sure the driver stopped, Henry stood in the middle of the road and waved his arms. The cabbie, Seth Adams, reined in his horse which halted less than a foot from Henry.

"Yer barmy bugger, what the hell do yer think yer playing at? Yer'll get yersen killed. Gerrout o t' road!"

Henry ignored the tirade. "Help me with this woman, she's badly hurt. We'll take her to Dr Chalmers in your cab." The cab driver's attitude instantly changed when he saw Dolly lying on the pavement, her face covered in blood. She was obviously in considerable pain. He climbed down from the cab. "It's Dolly from t' shop. Eh lass, we'll try not to hurt you." Henry and Seth, between them gently lifted Dolly into the back of the cab. Henry got in beside her and supported her against his shoulder, while Seth soon had his horse moving at a swift pace to Doctor Chalmers' surgery, which was luckily just around the corner. He drew up at the surgery door and went to help Henry lift Dolly from the cab.

"It's too late," said a shocked Henry. "She's gone," he whispered, as tears welled up in his eyes. "Are you sure?" but one look at Dolly convinced Seth, that she was indeed dead. He went into the surgery to summon help.

30

Stan Merriman had just started climbing up the open wooden stairs from the cellar, a flitch of bacon over his shoulder, when the trapdoor above him slammed shut, causing him to lose his balance and his hold on the bacon. "Shit!" he said as he picked himself up. Apart from a twisted ankle he wasn't hurt. Gingerly, trying not to put his full weight on his damaged ankle he climbed up again until he was high enough to reach the bottom of the trapdoor. He pushed with all his strength, but the door wouldn't budge. "Shit!" he said again, "something must have fallen on top." The cellar was dimly lit by an oil lamp suspended on a chain from the ceiling. He looked around to see if there was anything to use to push under the edge of the door and lever it up. There wasn't anything suitable. "Dolly should be back any minute," he said to himself. He shouted her name several times at the top of his voice. He could hear the muffled sound of gunfire, but nothing else. He realised that all he could do for the time being was to wait either for Dolly's return, or for a customer to come into the shop. He sat down on a sack of flour and waited, listening intently for any sound of footsteps from above, and occasionally calling out in the faint hope that someone might possibly hear him.

31

The shelling intensified. The hospital had never been so busy; everyone was working with a calm efficiency. The two nuns were proving to be worth their weight in gold, treating patients compassionately and professionally. Matron Richardson, pleasantly surprised at their obvious capability, was happy to leave them to work unsupervised. Indeed, she was gratified to note that all her staff, from the newest probationers to the senior sisters, were coping competently and quietly. It did not occur to the Matron that this efficiency was largely due to her capable training, the high standards she set for her staff and also to the excellent example she herself displayed. There was no sign of fear or panic, and if any member of staff was frightened they didn't show it. The bed shortage was a problem, but this was being overcome. Cots had been moved from the children's ward into the women's ward, and camp beds were set up in any available space. Many of the not too seriously ill patients were helping as best they could. The women patients looked after the children thus releasing the nurses for more important work. Several casualties, although bad enough to be admitted under normal conditions, elected to go home to recover, to free beds for the worst cases.

32

In all his years of working as a booking clerk, Freddie Atkinson had never sold as many tickets in a day as he had during the last fifteen minutes, and still the queue seemed endless. Billy Bowman knew that many people had pushed past him without a ticket, but what could he do? They'd be caught by the guard on the train or at the ticket barrier at their destination, he thought with satisfaction.

The cab drivers were doing a roaring trade. Usually at this time of day business was quiet, though fairly steady with regular customers, but now those who could afford them, to take them anywhere, as long as it was away from the bombing, had hired all the horse-drawn and motorised vehicles. Many of the horses, frightened by the flashes and the blasts, were difficult to control. Several customers didn't know where they wanted to go, as long as it was away from the sea. The roads leading towards York and Pickering were choc-a-bloc with all kinds of conveyances. Even at holiday times, there had never been such congestion. Tempers were lost when the faster motor vehicles were unable to overtake those that were horse-drawn or man-powered. Several people were on bicycles and tandems, and even more pedestrians were pushing overloaded carts and perambulators. No amount of shouting and threatening could make them move out of the way any faster.

33

Clive Weston, his younger sister Daisy, and their cousin Jane Cattle, lived quite a distance away in a small village just north of the town, which had no school of its own. They came to school by train each morning. One train got them there very early, nearly an hour before school started, but the next one didn't arrive until five minutes after lessons began. On the occasions that they'd missed the early train they had been caned and kept in after school, which meant they missed the train home and had to wait for nearly an hour for the next one. On fine days they played chasing games in the school playground, on wet days they sheltered in the school entrance, until it was time to line up with the other children before being marched into school. Sometimes, if the weather was especially bad, Charlie Jennings, the school caretaker, took pity on them and unlocked the door earlier than usual, to let them shelter in the cloakroom, but they had to go outside again before any teachers arrived. He found them, on this misty morning, huddled together in the entrance, cold and frightened by the shelling.

"Come on, you bairns." Charlie unlocked the door, but instead of leaving them in the cloakroom as usual, he took them to his basement boiler room, which was also his storeroom.

"Ye'll be all right here," he said, "I'll stay wi' ye."

"Thank you, Mr Jennings," chorused the children gratefully.

The next volley of shells destroyed the school hall, and the entrance in which Clive, Daisy and Jane had been sheltering only two minutes previously, causing widespread damage to other parts of the building too. Unaware of their close shave, the children quietly sat close together on a wooden packing case, holding hands. The noise of the shells was muffled in the boiler room, but they were warm now and felt safe. They were excited at being in Charlie's private domain, which was usually out of bounds to them. They couldn't wait to tell their schoolmates when they finally assembled for morning school.

34

Iris felt cold and miserable, as she stood under the pier with her mother and several neighbours. Matthew hadn't come back from Gran's yet, he must have decided to stay with her until all this was over. She hoped he was still at Gran's, and not in the open with the possibility of being hit by a shell or flying debris. Iris wondered how much longer it would go on: she had no sense of time, and seemed to have been standing in wet muddy sand for an eternity, she wouldn't have believed anyone who told she'd been there only about five minutes. If she'd got out of bed when her mother first called her, she'd have been dressed warmly instead of being in her nightie with just a coat over it, and only a pair of inadequate slippers on her frozen feet. Everyone else under the pier was cold and uncomfortable too, but Iris didn't think of that. All she could do was stand and shiver, wallow in self-pity and look forward to getting back to her mother's warm kitchen. That reminded her, she hadn't had any breakfast yet and she was hungry. The warships looked enormous from where she was standing, even though they were partly hidden by the sea wall. The flashes from their guns were vivid against the grey morning mist, the noise of the shells was deafening. She was unable to see the Foreshore from her position, but caught glimpses of the South Cliff, where several buildings were on fire. Under the pier seemed to be the safest place to be for the time being, even if it wasn't the most comfortable: the shells were aimed over and above them. The first volleys had concentrated on the sea-front, the Castle and the South Cliff, now the range was extended and the missiles were directed towards the town centre and beyond.

35

"Just wait here by the fire, darling, I've forgotten to bring you some clean knickers, how silly of me. I'll just be a minute, then I'll dress you and get you some breakfast." Lydia Charlton left her three-year-old daughter Elizabeth naked on the hearth rug, in front of the blazing fire, protected by a large mesh guard. The little girl stood looking at the flames, patiently waiting for her Mother to come back and dress her. A terrific explosion close by, frightened Elizabeth so much she screamed and ran out into the passage-way, where the blast had blown the front door open. In her panic, and still nude, Elizabeth ran out into the street and kept on running. She didn't know where she was going, she didn't feel cold at first, her body was still warm from the fire, but soon the damp mistiness cooled her and still running she started shivering.

"Little girl, little girl, what are you doing? Where are you going?" A middle-aged lady with a kind face caught up with her, Elizabeth shrieked and struggled. A pony and cart with about half a dozen children in it was on the side of the road nearby.

"It's all right, dear, I'm not going to hurt you. Where have you come from? Where's your Mother?" Elizabeth, too distressed to comprehend, sobbed and shivered, she stopped struggling, and lay limply in the lady's arms. The lady took off her thick coat and the long shapeless woollen cardigan that she wore under it. Elizabeth started to struggle again as she was wrapped in the cardigan, but soon ceased as the lady took the little girl in her arms and put her in the cart with the other children, who looked curiously at Elizabeth. Some of the children had sniggered at her nakedness, and now giggled at the sight of her bundled into a cardigan, which could envelop her three times over. In spite of the warm cardigan Elizabeth was still shivering, from fright as well as from cold. The lady replaced her coat and bade a child in the cart, who looked to be about ten years old:

"Kate, look after her, we'll find her mother as soon as we can."

"Yes, Mrs Butler," said Kate obediently. She tried to put her arms round Elizabeth, who shook her off and huddled down abjectly. The pony started off again, taking the children away from the shelling.

Lydia hurried downstairs, the front door was standing open, Elizabeth was nowhere to be seen. At first Lydia assumed that perhaps her daughter was playing 'hide-and-seek'. She called her name and looked behind the settee and under the table, she looked in the tiny scullery, which was not big enough to conceal a kitten, but there was no sign of Elizabeth. Lydia ran out into the street. There was a lot of debris, several houses in the street had been damaged, some slightly and some more severely. She didn't take this in, so concerned was she in finding her little girl. There were lots of people hurrying up the street, many of them with bundles of belongings. Lydia kept asking if anyone had seen a naked three-year-old girl, a few answered in the negative or shook their heads, but the majority didn't even bother to reply, so intent were they on escaping the bombardment. Shouting her little girl's name, Lydia ran frantically up the street, then down again, not knowing where to start looking for Elizabeth. She decided to follow the direction that most people were taking, but when she reached the end of the street, she didn't know which way to turn. Again she asked people if they'd seen her daughter, and eventually a man told her that Mrs Butler, the wife of the vicar of All Saints Church, had taken a group of children in a pony cart to a place of safety, but he didn't know exactly where to. He couldn't say whether Elizabeth was among the group, but it gave Lydia some hope. The man pointed in the direction in which the cart had gone and she ran, hoping to catch up with Mrs Butler before long, and praying that Elizabeth was with her.

36

Mrs Cherry, the cook at "Dunollie", stood in the hall with the rest of the staff, unable to take in what had happened, and not sure what to do. The two young maids were in no state to do anything, both were sobbing unrestrainedly, their arms around each other. Margaret's and Albert's bodies still lay at the front of the house. The staff, not knowing what to do, had rightly covered them with blankets, but they were in too much shock to know what to do next.

Cook became aware that she could hear the sound of a bell echoing up from the kitchen region. She realised it had been ringing for some time, but until now it had not penetrated her grief.

"Oh God! Lady Dorothea won't know what's happened." She slowly went upstairs, knocked briefly on Lady Dorothea's bedroom door and entered without waiting to be invited.

"Mrs Cherry?" The mistress was surprised to see her cook above stairs; she rarely left the kitchen during working hours. "What has happened? What are all those loud noises?"

"We're being bombarded from the sea, ma'am, half your house has been destroyed, Margaret and Albert are dead!" Cook spoke as if she were relaying her daily menu.

"Bombarded? Margaret dead? Who is Albert? How much damage is there? Has anyone informed Sir Robert?" Lady Dorothea was bemused, and her questions were largely rhetorical. Without waiting for cook to even think of replying, her ladyship pulled herself together quickly, sprang out of bed and began to dress.

"I'll be down in two minutes," she said. Mrs Cherry hastily withdrew, embarrassed by her mistress's lack of modesty. Lady Dorothea had few inhibitions, she was a forthright women in her late thirties, her husband Sir Robert was twelve years her senior and as staid as she was vivacious. Nevertheless, in spite of, or maybe because of their different personalities, they had a very happy and stable marriage. They had three sons who were away at school. Dorothea was looking forward to their homecoming in two days' time, for the Christmas holidays. The eldest, named Robert after his father, but called Bobby by the family, was a tall, good-looking lad of fifteen, his brothers Alistair and Alexander, referred to as Al and Lex by their peers, were twins who would be celebrating their thirteenth birthday in the New Year.

Dorothea was a good organiser, and she immediately took charge of the present situation. The staff were standing uncertainly in the hall near the bottom of the stairs, having been alerted by cook that Lady Dorothea was on her way down. She took in the situation immediately. First of all she ordered her husband's valet, Mr Gray, and Mr Featherstone the butler, with help from Mr Hodgson the elderly odd-job man, to bring the bodies inside the house, until such time as they could be removed to the mortuary. Margaret and Albert were laid reverently, side by side on the billiard table, and carefully covered with pristine white sheets, instead of the rough blankets that had previously covered them. Lady Dorothea cursorily examined the damage to the library, there was nothing she could do about that for the time being, but later in the morning, she would contact a builder, have the debris cleared and arrange for temporary repairs to be carried out. She telephoned an undertaker to arrange for Albert's and Margaret's bodies to be taken to a chapel of rest. Her next task was to contact her husband, but she realised that his train would not reach his office in London for another three or four hours yet, so she decided to wait until later in the morning, when he would have reached his destination and she could speak to him personally, rather than leave a message with someone she didn't know.

"Well, Mrs Cherry," said Dorothea, with a cheeriness she was far from feeling, when all the tasks had been completed, "what about a nice cup of tea and some toast for everyone?" Glad of something practical to do, Cook and the two maids withdrew to the kitchen where they were soon joined, not only by the rest of the staff but democratically, by the mistress as well. Nobody felt like talking, they were all in a state of shock, but the strong sweet tea helped a little to restore their spirits.

37

"Give me the child, bring him in here." Bill Williams slowed his pace, he looked at the man who had spoken to him, and recognised him as the local Methodist Minister.

"He's hurt his head, he was in t' backyard, t' Co-op's been blown up, some bricks and things came into t' yard and summat hit him. I'm taking him to t' hospital," Bill explained breathlessly as he tried to hurry on: the little boy was bleeding profusely from a wound on his head, and crying loudly with pain and fright.

The Minister stepped forward and said again: "Bring him in here, we have facilities and it's quite a step to the hospital." With a mixture of reluctance and relief Bill handed over his precious burden. The child was becoming heavier with each step he took.

"He'd just gone out to t' yard, when some shells hit the Co-op - our house is just behind it - some bits off it fell into our yard," Bill explained again. "I think there's somebody buried under t' main part in t' street. I'd have helped to dig 'em out if t' lad hadn't been hurt." He anxiously followed the minister down a corridor.

"What is the boy's name?" asked the Minister as he led the way into the schoolroom.

"Lewis - Lewis Williams," said Bill. "He's four years old," he added.

"I'm the Reverend Philip Taylor, I'm the minister of this church, as you'll undoubtedly know. We have set up an emergency first aid centre here. We have some qualified people, Dr Andrews has kindly offered his services, and there are two ladies who were trained nurses before their marriages. Any very serious cases that we are unable to give full treatment for we send to the main hospital. A member of my congregation has a motor car," he said proudly, as if he bore some of the credit for ownership of the vehicle. "He is very generously helping us by ferrying any patients to the hospital. Do not be afraid, the boy will be looked after here," Mr Taylor assured Bill, who now felt confident that Lewis was in capable hands.

The schoolroom in the basement of the church was set up as a first aid post. There were about half a dozen camp beds arranged round the walls, with a few people already receiving treatment. Apart from the doctor and the two nurses, easily identified by long white pinafores over blue dresses, there were several volunteers: one lady was carefully cleaning a wound on an old man's hand. Another was bandaging an arm wound. In one corner a few people were seated round a table and a formidable-looking lady was serving them cups of tea. "It's hot and sweet. Good for shock. Drink up!" she urged them heartily.

The Rev Taylor lay Lewis on the bed and signalled to the doctor, who came over immediately. He tenderly examined the wound to Lewis's head and checked him over for any other injuries. Dr Andrews looked at the boy's obviously worried father.

"Don't worry," he said kindly, "it's not as bad as it looks. There's a gash on his forehead, but it's not too deep, it doesn't even need a stitch, and there's some grazing on his cheek. Head wounds always bleed a lot, but once we've cleaned him up and put a dressing on, he should be all right. He'll probably have a headache for a while, but he'll soon be as good as new." The doctor patted Lewis reassuringly on the shoulder and signalled to one of the volunteers, murmured a few instructions to her, then went to see to the next casualty. Lewis's crying had by this time become hiccupping sobs. "Hullo! I'm Mrs Taylor," the cheerful-looking young woman, who was the Minister's wife, introduced herself as she came to carry out the doctor's orders. With professional competence she swiftly and gently cleaned Lewis's head wound, talking soothingly to him all the time. She soon had a neat dressing over the wound.

"There you are. A proper wounded soldier!" she said brightly, "now you go over there and the nice lady will give you a glass of milk, then you can go home and show your Mummy and tell her what a brave boy you are."

Bill thanked her, and took Lewis over to the table where he was given a glass of milk, which he drank greedily. Bill had a cup of tea, for which he was grateful, as he was now feeling weak with relief, and needed some sort of stimulant. The lady serving the refreshments informed Bill that the first aid group had been set up some time ago. They met once a week in the schoolroom of the church, had speakers and demonstrators, and practised bandaging and artificial respiration on each other, learned about pressure points, how to make a tourniquet and what to do in the case of shock. This was the first time they had been able to put all the theory into practice. Bill was very impressed with their efficiency. As soon their drinks were finished he thanked the doctor, the Reverend Taylor and the volunteer ladies, and took Lewis home, where his wife and three other children were waiting anxiously. Bill, an unemployed labourer, had offered to come back and help the volunteers in any capacity, so grateful was he for the help given to Lewis. The Reverend Taylor accepted the offer with gratitude and alacrity. Within ten minutes Bill had returned, having safely delivered Lewis to his relieved mother, who had been worrying all the time her husband and son were absent. She had been unable to leave her other children. Following instructions from the doctor, Bill was soon pulling his weight with the other volunteers. He learned quickly and found he was quite enjoying the work, in spite of the circumstances that had brought it about.

38

Mary Benson placed a bowl of porridge in front of each of her young sons, David and Edward. As her husband sat down she put three large rashers of bacon out of the frying pan onto a plate, added a couple of eggs, two sausages and a thick slice of fried bread, and set it down on the table in front of him. As he started eating, she poured out two mugs of strong tea, and put one in front of her husband; the other was for her eldest son Christopher, home on leave from the Navy. She put a couple of rashers of bacon between two slices of bread to take upstairs to Chris.

"You're spoiling that lad, Mary!" said her husband, indistinctly, his mouth full of sausage.

"Oh Sam, it's only that it's his last day here. Just think of the hardships he might have to face. He won't be having breakfast in bed for a long, long time."

"Aye," said Sam dryly and turned his attention back to his breakfast.

"Just listen to that shooting or whatever it is, it seems to be getting nearer. Out of the way, Timmy," said Mary, as with her foot she gently nudged the black and white cat, which was rubbing himself against the leg of her chair. Timmy me-owed indignantly and ambled to the hearth rug where he stretched himself in front of the fire, and started washing his paws.

"It's them bloody Germans," said Sam. Without moving from his chair he bawled up to Christopher to come downstairs. Mary was just about to pick up the mug of tea from the table, when a large explosion nearby shook the house like an earthquake. Mary ran round the table and protectively took her children in her arms. The next explosion destroyed most of the house, completely burying them all under a pile of bricks.

This was the last day of Able Seaman Christopher Benson's

leave; he would be going back to his base on the three o'clock train that afternoon. It was his first leave after training, and probably the last in the foreseeable future. He had joined the Royal Navy within a few days of the outbreak of war, much to his mother's dismay. He didn't yet know to which ship he had been assigned, or where he would be going. His mother would worry anyway - even if he was shore-based, she would worry about him. David and Edward, Chris's little brothers, were, fortunately, far too young at eight and five to be involved in a war, even if it should go on for a year or two, and she was grateful for that at least. Mary Benson had hoped her eldest son would be spending Christmas at home and was very disappointed that his leave hadn't worked out more favourably. Because it was his last day, Christopher was having a lie-in. He had heard the gun-fire in the distance and assumed it was maybe some exercise going on, out at sea. He was rather disgruntled that it had started so early in the morning, and disturbed him. After a few minutes the noise stopped, Chris turned over and snuggled down in the bed again. He could hear the murmur of voices in the kitchen below as his mother prepared breakfast for his father and the two youngsters. The gunfire started again, this time it was much nearer. He heard his father shout up to him:

"Come away downstairs, lad, it's t' Germans!" Chris laughed to himself and turned over in bed, his dad was just trying to get him up. He was startled when there was an explosion directly above his head. Chris jumped out of bed in one movement and rapidly began to dress, he had just put on his shirt over his long woollen underpants when there was an almighty crash and the floor gave way beneath him, catapulting him into the kitchen. Christopher was stunned for what seemed an age, dazedly he looked around: the house was open to the street, and he could see no sign of his parents or his brothers. When he'd partially recovered his wits, he began frantically to move some of the rubble. He called to some people passing by to help, but they ignored him and did not stop.

"Help me, help me, please! There are two bairns under here with my Mam and Dad. Please help," Chris pleaded, as he carried on digging wildly with his bare hands. Some of the passers-by even laughed and jeered at Chris's state of undress.

"Where's your trousers then? What nice legs you've got!" Chris didn't hear them, but Mrs Davison, who lived opposite, did. She had just helped her elderly partially sighted husband down the stairs of their damaged house. She seated him on a stool in the cupboard under the stairs, where she hoped he would be protected and safe.

"Stay there, Pat love, I won't be long." Pat smiled trustingly, and like an obedient child did as he was told and sat quietly waiting for her return.

Kathleen ran across the road to her neighbours' house, wrathfully berating the unheeding public. "You rotten bastards, can't you see the lad's trying to find his little brothers? What kind of people are you?" She screeched at Chris's tormentors, she lashed out at those nearest to her, and then she began digging in the rubble with her bare hands, alongside the desperate young sailor. A couple of men, shamed by her words, did stop and start helping, then two young territorials ran up and started shifting the rubble. Somehow, Sam had managed to pull himself painfully out of the debris. He was quite badly injured and in considerable distress, his face was bleeding. Sam brushed dust and blood away from his eyes, and with Chris and the two territorials, tugged at the bricks with his already bleeding hands.

Christopher found his mother, with her left arm around David, and her right arm clutching Edward: she was alive and groaning softly. The front of her pinafore was saturated with blood. With horror, Christopher saw that her right hand was missing. He didn't know what to do. One of the territorials took off his belt and wrapped it round Mary's arm to make a rough tourniquet. But it was too late, Mary died even before the man's attempts at first aid were complete.

It seemed a long time, but was only a few minutes, before a team of rescuers arrived. They gently released Edward: he was alive, but unconscious. They pulled David's crushed little body out a few minutes later. An ambulance arrived, the crew working quickly and efficiently wrapped Edward up, and gently put him into the ambulance, then placed a protesting Mr Benson onto a stretcher and put him next to Edward. As the ambulance drove away two of the rescuers gently laid Mary's and David's bodies on the pavement and covered them with blankets, to await a hearse to take them to the mortuary. Someone put a blanket around Chris's shoulder. He seemed unaware of what was going on, his face was blank and his eyes unseeing.

"Come lad," said a quiet voice, "you need some treatment too, let's get you to hospital."

Chris resisted at first, he wanted to stay with his mother and David, but when he was persuaded there was nothing he could do for either of them he allowed himself to be gently led away. He didn't seem to realise that he too had been injured. He had broken an arm in the fall through the ceiling, but had ignored the pain in his frantic attempts to rescue his family. There was a deep gash in his other arm and a large cut on his head, another on his cheek and cuts to his feet, and there was extensive bruising all over his body. When he reached the hospital, the news was gently broken to Chris that Edward had died in the ambulance, and that Sam was in a critical condition, his injuries more severe than they had at first appeared. Christopher was completely uncomprehending, he didn't say a word, he was in deep shock. He sat passively while a nun and a young nurse tended his injuries. He showed no surprise at seeing a nun working in the hospital. He showed absolutely no emotion at all. He seemed anaesthetised, giving little sign of the pain he must have been in, apart from flinching occasionally as his wounds were cleaned and dressed.

39

"We must have been here hours and hours," thought Iris, still huddled under the pier. "I'll never be warm again." The noise of the gunfire seemed to get louder and louder by the minute. Her head ached, and she'd never felt so miserable. Then, suddenly, the shelling stopped. Iris heard someone say, "T' buggers are going." As the group of people under the pier waited, the ships began to turn and head out to sea. Before they sailed away in convoy, the last ship in the line, in a final defiant act, fired a volley of shells at the Lighthouse.

Iris watched in fascination, as the glass dome at the top of the Lighthouse seemed to fall, in slow motion, into the sea. It seemed to take an age to complete the descent: it moved in a slow arc, then it hit the water with a loud splash and sent spray twenty feet into the air. Within minutes, the whole of the dome had vanished under the surface of the sea. The German warships had disappeared into the mist. Mrs Appleby and her neighbours didn't move for a few seconds, then stiffly, they stretched their frozen limbs.

"It looks as if it's all over," Iris heard Mrs Holton say. "Aye, I think it'll be safe enough to go home again now," replied her husband. Mr Holton had a wooden leg as the result of an accident he'd had at sea many years ago. "At least that one won't be cold," thought Iris irreverently.

"You don't think they might come back, Alf?" Mrs Holton asked her husband.

"Nay, they've done their damage," he replied grimly, and led the way up the slipway on to the road.

Stiffly the band of neighbours followed him, with many a backward glance towards the sea, where the German warships were now out of sight. The acrid smell of gun smoke was still in the air. The mist was beginning to clear, revealing the scenes of devastation. The group separated, anxious to get home to see what damage, if any, had been done to their properties. Iris glanced up at the clock on the parish church, high on the hill above them: it showed the time as half past eight. "It must have stopped," she thought, "we've been under that wharf for hours." But even as she was thinking it, the clock struck the half hour. As they were crossing the road, Iris realised that one of the new shoes she'd been holding during their sojourn under the pier, was missing. With a brief word to her mother she ran back across the road, down under the pier, and poked about in the wet sand, but there was no sign of the shoe. She retraced her steps twice, but she still couldn't find it. Sadly, she went home, to find that Mrs Appleby had poked up the fire into a roaring blaze, so that the kitchen was warm and welcoming.

"I've lost one of my shoes, one of my brand-new shoes," wailed Iris, as she entered. A sharp stinging slap on her cheek startled her into a stunned silence.

"Lost your shoe? Lost your flaming shoe?" her mother screamed at her. "Just think yourself lucky that's all you've lost. Young Raymond has lost his *foot*, and Mrs Harrison has lost her little boy. God knows how many other people have lost relatives and limbs, and you whine because you've lost a shoe! You'd no business taking them out, anyroad, you're not having another pair," she vowed as she turned away, dabbing her eyes with the corner of her pinny.

Iris felt ashamed. Her mother was right, what was the loss of a shoe compared with loss of life, or loss of a foot. She also felt embarrassed, she'd never seen her mother cry before, and didn't know what to do; she just stood in silence. The tears slowly rolling down her cheeks had little to do with the pain of the circulation returning to her hands and feet or to the effects of the slap on her cheek. Mrs Appleby busied herself at the kitchen range, then turned and set a steaming dish of porridge on the table, poured some thick cream over it and ordered Iris to: "Get that down you, it'll warm you up," as if nothing had happened. Gratefully, Iris sat down and slowly began to eat. As her mother had predicted, she soon began to feel warm again. But the feeling of shame took longer to subside.

40

Richard Lovell had watched the bombardment from beginning to end, frustrated that he could do nothing to help. Ruth went to see how the children and their nanny were. Nanny was quite nervous but was bravely trying not to show it. The children seemed unconcerned; they had just got out of bed and were not yet dressed. The nursery windows faced away from the sea, so they were probably as safe there as anywhere. Ruth rejoined Richard; it didn't occur to either of them that the large windows would be an easy target if the shells were aimed in the direction of the house. Luckily for them the shells were being directed towards the main part of the town. From their elevated position they could see fires in various locations, all over the area, and a thick cloud of smoke hovered above like a menacing shadow.

"They're going," said Richard, as the firing suddenly stopped and the ships turned and moved slowly out to sea. But, even as he spoke, he saw a gaping hole appear in the side of the lighthouse, and the dome keeled over into the sea as a final salvo was fired from the *Kolberg,* the last of the three ships to depart.

"They're going," Richard repeated. "Thank God! What a despicable thing to do," he added furiously. "Firing on innocent civilians, that's not an act of war, it's an atrocity!"

"Richard, look!" Ruth pointed down the cliff: there was a woman with a little dog, who seemed to be searching for something. "I think she must be the wife of the man who fell over the cliff. It's the same dog. I'll go to her." Ruth left the room and a few moments later Richard saw her talking earnestly to the woman. He saw Ruth put an arm around her shoulder and lead her away. He sighed, and yet again wished he wasn't so helpless.

41

Stella hovered between unconsciousness, and a vague awareness of some sort of activity going on around her. Her body was one mass of pain, but the pain was strangely disembodied as if she was feeling it for someone else. She groaned, and heard a soothing voice tell her: "Hold on a bit longer, love, we'll have you out soon." She didn't understand. Out? Out where? She had no idea where she was or what had happened. Her head hurt too much to try and work it out and she lapsed into unconsciousness again.

The rescuers had been carefully digging through the rubble for twenty minutes. They had found Anne first: her body was broken and crushed, but her face was surprisingly undamaged and serene in death. They had thought that Stella was dead too when they first reached her, but a slight moan indicated that there was some life at least. As they uncovered her they knew her injuries were severe. The men were attempting to gently lift a large piece of masonry from Stella's right leg, trying not to hurt her more than was necessary. She screamed as the object was finally removed, and mercifully lapsed into deep unconsciousness again. Very slowly and painstakingly, so as not to jolt her more than was necessary, Stella was placed onto a stretcher, and conveyed with great care to the waiting ambulance, which was soon on its way, bell ringing urgently, to the hospital.

"I reckon she'll lose that leg," said Frank Porter, as he wiped some of the dust and sweat from his face.

"Aye, if she lives," replied Bob West, and the other men nodded in agreement. "Let's see to this young woman," he added. They turned back to the distressing task of removing Anne's body from the rubble.

42

Audrey Thompkinson had spent most of the duration of the bombardment huddled in a chair, with her head bent and her hands over her ears shaking with fright. The shelling had started several minutes after Geoffrey had left. It took her a few moments to realise that the noise had ceased and had been replaced by a new sound: she could hear Jasper. Feeling relieved, Audrey went to open the door to Geoffrey, but he wasn't there. There was only Jasper, barking frantically, and her relief turned to alarm. The little dog ran towards her, then back to the gate: she realised he wanted her to follow him and knew that something had happened to Geoffrey. Snatching a coat from the hallstand she followed the little dog. Jasper led her to the cliffs, but there was still no sign of her husband. The dog was getting more and more frenzied:

he kept running to the edge of the cliff and back to Audrey. Cautiously she approached the cliff and looked down onto the rocks below, fearful of what she would discover. She couldn't see anything, other than the sea washing angrily over the rocks. Agitatedly she turned away, not knowing what to do, then she saw a young woman hurrying along the cliff path towards her.

"Are you looking for someone?" asked Ruth Jenkins, she wasn't sure how to approach this distressed woman, knowing that she was probably the bearer of bad news.

"My husband hasn't come back from his morning walk. My dog is acting peculiarly and I thought Geoffrey might have had an accident." The usually reticent Audrey wouldn't normally speak to a complete stranger like this, but her panic made her voluble.

"Oh, my dear." Ruth took Audrey's arm compassionately and gently told her what she and Richard had seen from their window.

"My employer alerted the authorities, and they were to send a boat out to search the area." Audrey stared uncomprehendingly at Ruth, unable to take in what she was saying.

"Come, I'll take you home and stay with you until we hear some news. Have you someone who can be with you?" Audrey didn't reply: her face was blank, her eyes lacklustre, as she let Ruth gently lead her away.

Richard watched through his telescope as the two women disappeared from sight. He knew Ruth would stay with the other woman as long as necessary. He trained his telescope towards the pier slip way and saw a boat pulling away, there were three men in it. Richard recognised it as the inshore search and rescue boat, he wondered what they would find.

43

Despite the chill of the morning and even though she was not wearing a coat, Lydia Charlton felt hot and flustered. In her thin slippers she had covered more than a mile in her frantic search for her daughter. She had a stitch in her side and was out of breath. Lydia hadn't told anyone yet, but she was pregnant, she'd only known for sure herself a few days previously, and wanted her husband Paul to be the first to know, but he was away at sea, and wouldn't home for another three weeks. How she wished he was here now, this would never have happened, Elizabeth would have been safe. What would Paul say when he found his little daughter was missing? How was Lydia going to explain to him? She was getting more and more agitated, when ahead of her she saw the Church and the group of houses that made up the small quiet village of Scalby . There seemed to be a lot of activity near the Church Hall. Lydia hurried inside; the large room seemed to be full of people, mostly children, many of whom were crying. Anxiously surveying the various groups Lydia suddenly caught sight of Elizabeth wrapped in a shapeless cardigan. With a cry of joy, she pushed her way across the room and took the little girl in her arms. Elizabeth began to cry again as Lydia hugged her tightly. The vicar's wife hurried over.

"Are you her mother?" she asked. The question was rhetorical the answer was obvious. "Come over here and sit down, dear," she said kindly, "you look all in. She is quite safe and you mustn't distress yourself in your condition."

"How did you know?" Lydia was astonished, as there was no visible sign of her pregnancy.

"Oh, I can always tell," said Mrs Butler briskly, without explaining how. "Sit down here, dear, I expect you could do with a cup of tea, then I'll see if I can find someone to take you both home."

She did not question how a three-year-old child came to be running naked in the street on a cold December morning. There were other things to occupy the vicar's wife, she was trying to get some semblance of order out of chaos, and was actually succeeding.

Lydia wearily sank down in the chair Mrs Butler had indicated, and held Elizabeth close to her breast. The child contentedly snuggled up to her mother, stuck her thumb in her mouth and promptly fell asleep.

44

The three injured members of the Benson family had been taken to hospital, and the bodies of Mary and David Benson had been taken away in a hearse. Kathleen Davison watched until the ambulance was out of sight, before she crossed the road to her own home: she had all but forgotten her husband, sitting uncomplaining in the cupboard under the stairs. He smiled happily as he heard her come into the house, showing several gaps where teeth were missing.

"Oh Patrick, oh love." Kathleen couldn't control her tears as she led him out of the cupboard into the kitchen. Pat put his arm around her shoulders.

"Don't worry, love," he said comfortingly, "don't you fret, lass, he'll come back, he's just wandered off, I reckon, but he'll come back." For a moment Kathleen was puzzled, not understanding what he was talking about, then she remembered. Her poor dear husband, who was unable to recall incidents that had happened a few minutes ago, was referring to an event that had happened nearly fifty years ago, when she was eighteen and he a year or two older, before they were married. Kathleen's little dog had gone missing and she had been very distressed, Patrick had said those very words to her at the time: "Don't worry, love, he'll come back." He was right: a day or two later, covered in dust and cobwebs, Rudie had arrived back home; no-one ever knew where he'd been, and Rudie was not telling. There was no happy ending this time, though. Kathleen knew that she would never forget the sight of her neighbour, who had been such a good friend to her, lying on the pavement with her little boy by her side. Patrick, living in his own little world, was blissfully unaware of the destruction that had gone on around them. Apart from Kathleen, Mary Benson was the only person that Patrick recognised these days: he didn't know his own family now, and asked "Who's that young feller?" or "Who's the pretty girl?" whenever one of his children or grandchildren came to visit. Mary came over most days to help Kathleen to wash and dress Pat. It was a time-consuming operation: as fast as his buttons were being fastened, Patrick would undo them, laughing like a mischievous child as he did so. He also needed help with feeding, Mary was a big help and had so much patience. Kathleen was getting old and hadn't the stamina to cope any more.

"The Lord knows how I'm going to manage without her," Kathleen thought, as the tears welled up in her eyes again. Patrick's eyesight was too bad to notice her distress. His immediate interest was concentrated on the spoonfuls of porridge his wife was feeding him, as if he was a baby. Kathleen knew her daughters and daughters-in-law were willing to help, but Patrick shied away from everyone who came near him, with the exception of his wife and Mary Benson, and anyway, their own families kept them busy. Kathleen almost envied her husband; in his cocoon of oblivion, he was quite happy, completely unmindful of everything going on around him. Not for him the pain of bereavement. Tenderly, Kathleen wiped Pat's face, then she gently led him to an armchair near the fire and handed him a piece of knitting. During his long hours at sea, Pat used to knit intricately patterned ganseys, now he contentedly knitted plain strips with many dropped stitches. When they got too long, Kathleen would pull them out and he'd start again. After she'd got him settled, Kathleen tackled her household tasks with a ferocious burst of energy. She knew she had to keep busy to stop herself dwelling on what had happened to her neighbours. She still felt very wrathful about the behaviour of the passers-by who had jeered at Christopher, when they should have been helping him. As she worked, she muttered curses under her breath. Patrick just smiled at her.

45

Dora Stafford had arrived home. She lived just round the corner from the hospital, and in normal circumstances it would take about three minutes at an average walking pace. It had taken Dora nearly ten. The staff had not allowed her to leave the hospital while the bombardment was at its height: she had been sitting in an uncomfortable dreary waiting room with some other patients, until the risk had minimised. When it was safe to leave, Dora set off, but had gone only a few yards when she realised that perhaps she wasn't as well as she'd thought. Stopping frequently, she arrived home almost in a state of collapse. There was no sign of any of her family when she arrived at the house. The unlocked door opened from the street, straight into the living room. Dora groaned as she looked round, she had been in hospital for two weeks, and during that time it was obvious that no attempt had been made to keep the place clean and tidy. The dust lay thickly on the shabby furniture; there were dirty cups and plates on the hearth and on the floor. She briefly looked into the kitchen; it was also in a terrible mess. Dora shut the door on it and returned to the living room; she flopped down on the only comfortable chair in the house. She was beginning to wish she'd taken Sister Fenton's advice and stayed in hospital. She was itching to start on cleaning the house, but she felt too tired and too poorly to do anything at present. Perhaps when she'd had a little rest, she might feel able to tackle it. She could do with a cup of tea, but didn't have the strength to go into the kitchen, wash a cup, and make one. The sudden opening of the door startled her: it was Bella Milton, her next-door neighbour.

"'Ee, Dora, I thought I saw you come in. 'Ee lass, you look terrible. I'm surprised they let you come out of hospital, you don't look well enough." Dora explained about the bed situation and how she'd insisted on discharging herself.

"But I wish I hadn't, Bella love. I was quite enjoying it in there, being waited on an 'all. It was like a holiday." Dora had never had a holiday in her life, and was unlikely to ever have one. "But I reckon there were a lot of poor souls needing a bed more than I did. Now look what I've come back to. Where's Ernie and t' kids? Anyroad, how did you get on through t' shelling?"

"They've gone down to t' Market Vaults, half o' t' neighbourhood are there, thinking it'd be safe from t' bombing," Bella answered her first question. "I decided I was just as safe in me own home as anywhere else. Now let's have a cup of tea - you look as if you need one." Dora nodded gratefully and hoped her family wouldn't come home too soon.

46

Alfie Ingleby couldn't believe his luck. The street, normally lined with cabs waiting for hire was deserted. Not a soul in sight, and not a window left intact in the jewellers! The whole of the front of the shop blown out and all its contents accessible, just waiting for someone like Alfie to take whatever he could carry. The little thief wasted no time in filling his pockets with rings, watches, necklaces and any other small objects he could cram in. Alfie was a small-time, not very successful crook: his forte was shop-lifting, but he did a bit of pick pocketing on the side, specialising in any place that was likely to be crowded. Scarborough in midsummer was quite a lucrative venue, with all the toffs congregating in the area of the Spa. The cricket festival in September was another good time for easy pickings.

He wasn't all that good at his job: having been caught several times he'd served a few jail sentences. In fact Alfie had been released from his latest sojourn as a guest at His Majesty's pleasure, only two days earlier. Alfie often wondered what pleasure His Majesty derived from it - none of his guests had any! He'd reasoned that the bombardment might provide him with opportunity; the police would be otherwise engaged and not have time to bother with the likes of him, but he hadn't expected such an open invitation. He filled the deep pockets of his overcoat, and the concealed pockets inside the lining, with as much as they could hold, then he tried to walk casually away. It was difficult, the loot was quite heavy, but he had no intention of putting any back. As Alfie hurriedly walked past the next shop, which was a newsagents he thought he heard something. He stopped and listened intently - yes, there it was again; someone was calling. Although not very quick-witted, even Alfie realised there was someone trapped inside, and it put him in a quandary: should he ignore the cries? Should he try and rescue the victim or should he go for help? His first instinct was to scarper quickly, but strangely enough he had a conscience of sorts and felt he ought to help. He soon decided against going for assistance: he was known to all the local bobbies and they would automatically be suspicious and no doubt, notice his bulging pockets. Alfie started shifting some of the debris away from the doorway of the shop, his heavy overcoat hampered him, but under no circumstances would he discard it! He was soon sweating with the unaccustomed exertion.

"Well, well, well! What have we here?" The familiar voice startled him.

"Oh, Mr Hardcastle, sir, some poor bugger's buried under all this rubbish, I was trying to dig him out, he might be injured." Alfie tried to sound like a virtuous citizen doing his duty, but only succeed in sounding guilty.

PC Derek Hardcastle had been surveying the area to ascertain what damage had been done and where there were likely to be people injured and buried under debris, so he could report back to the police station, and arrange for help where necessary. He had come across Alfie purely by chance. He immediately joined the little thief in his rescue work and soon they had enough debris cleared for them to reveal a man and a young girl.

"Are you hurt?" asked Derek.

"Don't think so, constable, a few bruises I reckon, but nowt broken. How about you, Nora lass?" he asked his young companion.

"I think I'm all right, Mr Patterson," Nora replied.

"Good girl," he said approvingly, then turned to their rescuers.

"We weren't actually hit by anything, just trapped inside by all these bricks blocking the door," Mr Patterson explained. "I'd like to get the shop open, just in case we have some customers."

"The enemy ships have sailed away, should get back to near normal soon," confirmed the constable, impressed by the determination to carry on he'd witnessed from so many people this morning.

"Alfie! where do you think you're going?" Derek said sharply, as the little man sidled away.

"Well, they're all right, Mr Hardcastle sir, I'll just be on my way."

"Those pockets look unusually heavy, what have you got in them? I think you'd better be going my way, Alfie, come along quietly now!"

Alfie gave a deep sigh, there was no point in resisting, he'd been caught again, and all because he'd tried to help a fellow human being. Life was so unfair.

47

At Doctor Chalmer's request, Seth Adams and Henry Pike had taken Dolly's body to the undertaker's on the opposite side of the street to Merriman's grocery shop. The doctor had confirmed that Dolly was indeed dead. He himself was rushed off his feet with, in addition to his normally busy surgery, many bombardment victims clamouring for his attention. To his relief, Seth and Henry agreed to go and break the news to Stan after they had been to the undertaker's. The doctor promised to call in at the shop as soon as he was free to do so.

"Stan?" called Seth.

"Stan! His name's Stan! That's what she said," Henry remembered.

"Eh? What are you talking about? STAN!" Seth raised his voice.

"Well, I thought she was saying "stand" you see, I thought she wanted to stand up, but she couldn't. She was really saying "Stan", you see, she was talking about her husband, that's what she was saying."

"Aye, well we'd better find t' poor bugger," Seth cut short Henry's ramblings.

Stan heard his name being called and the sound of feet above him, he shouted again. He was no longer competing with the sound of gunfire, so there was every chance that he would be heard. Seth and Henry looked around the shambles of the shop. There was flour all over the floor from a sack that had burst open, mixed with broken eggs and tinned goods that had fallen off the shelves. There was no sign of the owner, then faintly from beneath their feet they heard faint calls for help.

"He must be in t' cellar." Seth immediately began clearing away the spoiled merchandise from where he knew the trap door was located. Henry came to his aid and between them they soon had the door uncovered. Stan slowly and painfully climbed up the wooden steps and emerged from the darkness of the cellar, relieved to see daylight again. His ankle was quite swollen, but he was otherwise uninjured.

"Thanks, lads," he said to his rescuers. Supporting himself on the side of the counter he surveyed his store. "Bloody hell, what a mess," he continued. "I don't know where our Dolly's got to, she went to see if the Smiths were all right, she's been gone ages." He broke off, suspecting something was wrong, as he noticed the expressions on Seth's and Henry's faces. "Sit down, lad," said Seth gently, as he led Stan to the chair by the counter, reserved for customers waiting to be served. Awkwardly, Seth told Stan what had happened. For a moment Stan sat quietly, saying nothing, then angrily he rose to his feet and picking up the nearest thing to hand, which happened to be a large round cheese, he flung it at the opposite wall, it slithered down the wall leaving a creamy trail. He continued wildly throwing anything that came to hand, Henry moved forward to restrain him, but Seth gestured for him to wait. Seth knew that the grocer needed to do something to express his immediate grief. Within a few minutes as Seth had surmised, Stan's rage subsided. He sank down onto the chair again and with his head in his hands sobbed uncontrollably. Henry patted Stan's shoulder helplessly, not knowing what to do or what to say, to give the newly bereaved man any comfort. When eventually, Stan had calmed down a little, he asked where Dolly was. He insisted on seeing her straightaway: Seth and Henry tried to dissuade him and urged him to close the shop for the time being and go to his flat upstairs. But Stan was adamant, so Seth and Henry accompanied him across the road to Mr Bosley, the undertaker. Unlike the popular conception of an undertaker, Mr Bosley was a jolly-looking man, his appearance belying his occupation. He was however very sensitive to the feelings of the bereaved that he dealt with. He was reluctant to let Stan view Dolly's body at this stage, as he had not yet had time to prepare her in any way. Her face was still covered in blood, her clothes dishevelled and soiled, but Stan was so insistent, Mr Bosley feared he might fly into a rage. He led the three men into a room at the rear of the building, where Dolly lay on a marble slab. With a strangled cry Stan hurried forward, he took Dolly's hand and standing quietly, held it tightly for a few moments. He bent and kissed the dead face of his wife, then turned away quickly and left abruptly.

"Come back later, lad, I'll make her look right pretty," said Mr Bosley as Stan walked swiftly past him. Stan nodded briefly but didn't reply. He went back to his shop and immediately began clearing up the mess, refusing any help from Henry and Seth. Realising he needed to work hard to try and assuage his grief alone, the two men left him to it, promising to return later.

48

Despite the journey being up-hill all the way, the group of men and boys pushing Raymond on the handcart arrived at the hospital quite quickly. Panting and red-faced from the unaccustomed exertion, they ran into the hospital casualty department, handcart and all.

"You can't bring that in here. Take it outside," a man in a white coat officiously told them.

"Let us take the patient first," said a calm quiet voice. Raymond's father looked up into the face of a nun; she smiled at him.

"Lift the child onto this couch, please," she instructed, "as carefully as you can." Mr Turner and two of his fellow helpers cautiously lifted Raymond from the handcart onto the couch. Without being told, all the helpers went outside with the handcart and stood in the hospital forecourt to wait for Mr Turner, and further news of Raymond.

Sister Frances, after a quick but detailed look at Raymond's injuries, called Doctor Conroy over. He examined the little boy thoroughly.

"Who put this tourniquet on?" he asked Raymond's dad.

"It were a neighbour, Daniel Hudson."

"Well, he did a damned good job. The lad would have lost a lot more blood without it. It may even have saved his life. But the child's injuries are very severe, and I am afraid it looks as if we'll have to amputate that foot."

"You do whatever's right," replied Joe Turner looking anguished, but trusting the doctor's judgement and skills.

Doctor Conroy immediately gave orders for Raymond to be prepared for surgery.

"We'll do our very best for him," he assured the anxious father.

Joe went outside to tell Percy and the others what was happening.

"Will you go and tell his Mam for me?" he asked Percy.

"Aye! I'll bring her up later," was the reply.

Thanking Percy for the loan of his cart, Joe went back into the hospital, set for a long anxious wait. The boys and men, with Percy pushing his handcart, went back to Oxley's Yard to let everyone know what was happening at the hospital.

49

"Yes, but where on South Cliff does this Miss Fox live?" Ben asked Brian. "It's a big area, lad. Do you know the name of the street?" Brian thought hard, he wasn't sure if his mother had ever mentioned the name, then suddenly he remembered. "West Street!" he shouted triumphantly.

"West Street?" groaned Ben, "that's about the longest street there is. I don't suppose you know what number?" Brian shook his head. Colin had already left the group and gone home to change and hurry to the small preparatory school where he taught. Ben and Maurice had promised not only to find Brian and Donald's mother, but to go with Andy and explain to his employer what had happened to the delivery cart. Both young men were employed in firms owned by their respective fathers. Ben was a trainee accountant and Maurice a junior solicitor, and they could get away with being late for work occasionally - neither abused the privilege, but today was a rare exception, the circumstances were unique.

But they were having trouble in finding Mrs Hollis because the boys didn't know the address of their mother's employer.

"It's a big house," said Brian helpfully. Ben groaned again: all the houses in West Street could be described as 'big'.

"Thanks, that's a lot of help," he said wryly.

"Let's just knock on a few doors and ask if anyone knows a Miss Fox," suggested Maurice. Andy and Maurice took one side of the street and Ben, Brian and Donald took the other. It wasn't long before they found someone who knew Miss Fox and who was able to give them the number of the house. Brian and Donald were very impressed by the appearance of the house where their mother worked, they'd never been to this part of the town before. It was Mrs Hollis herself, with a feather duster in her hand, that answered the door. She gave a little shriek when she saw her two sons standing on the doorstep with Ben.

"What are you doing here? Have you been wandering about in that bombing?" Ben explained what had happened, bade farewell to the two little boys and raising his hat to Mrs Hollis, left with Maurice and Andy in tow. Sarah Hollis was so flustered she didn't think to thank him. She had been extremely worried about them, wondering if they had taken shelter somewhere, or if her house had been hit by shells and the boys injured or dead. Had she known they'd been outside in the thick of it she'd have been out of her mind with anxiety. She drew them into the large hallway and hugged them, as a querulous voice from a room on the right called out:

"Mrs Hollis, who is there?"

"I'm coming, Miss Fox," Sarah answered. "Stay there," she hissed at the two boys, "and be quiet." Miss Fox wanted to know who had called at such an unusually early hour. Sarah told her what had happened and apologised for her sons' unannounced arrival.

"I'll send them straight off to school, now the danger seems to be over," she said. "Nonsense! I'd like to meet them. Bring them in here," ordered Miss Fox. "They're already late for school, they may as well have the morning off at least. I doubt that the schools will be very well attended to day. Don't you agree?"

Surprised, Sarah did as she was bid and nervously ushered Brian and Donald into the drawing room. Miss Fox regarded them severely for a few moments.

"Sit down there," she ordered, pointing to a horse-hair sofa. They sat down abruptly, overawed by the unaccustomed ornateness of the large room, and by the ferocity of Miss Fox's manner. The sofa felt itchy to their bare legs, and it made a squeaky noise every time they moved, so they tried to sit perfectly still.

"Mrs Hollis, fetch two glasses of milk and some biscuits. Now then, you two, tell me how you got here and why you have come." Shyly at first, Brian with interruptions from Donald, was soon eagerly telling Miss Fox of his decision to find their mother after being told by a lady that the Germans were coming to get them. When Sarah returned to the drawing room with the milk and biscuits she was astonished to find her grumpy employer and her sons in animated conversation. What Sarah, or everyone else, hadn't realised, was that the old lady was lonely and bored with her own company, and that she welcomed the diversion the boys provided.

~

Miss Fox had been given the forenames Desdemona Ophelia Hermione by her mother, who was an avid admirer of Shakespeare. In spite of such grand names she had usually been called Mona by her parents; her brothers gave her the acronym Doh, which inevitably degenerated to Dodo. Miss Fox often wished her mother had called her after more conventionally-named Shakespearean heroines, like Rosalind or Juliet. Her two older brothers were uncompromisingly named Oliver and Charles by their father, who had studied the period of the Civil War in great detail, but was unable to decide which side he would have supported had he been involved in it. Impartially he had christened his sons after the two leading protagonists. The two brothers had died several years ago within six months of each other, neither of them having married; Miss Fox had inherited their accumulated wealth in addition to that left by their parents. She was a very rich lady, with little to spend her money on. For a long time now Desdemona Ophelia Hermione had not been called anything other than Miss Fox, and she'd almost forgotten the names she had been given. She lived alone in the family home that was much too large for her. Her needs were few and therefore she employed the minimum number of staff. Mrs Barton, the cook/housekeeper, lived in the basement flat with her husband, who pursued his own trade as a painter during normal working hours, and at other times acted as unpaid porter/handyman, in return for rent-free accommodation. Sarah Hollis did the cleaning two or three hours each morning, except Sundays, and a Mrs Ferris collected Miss Fox's household and personal laundry every Monday morning and returned it clean, aired and neatly ironed each Thursday afternoon. Miss Fox had a constant routine. She rose at seven-thirty each morning, Mrs Barton served her breakfast in the morning room at eight, she then read the morning papers in the drawing room. Afterwards, weather permitting, Miss Fox walked the length of the Esplanade, her back always as straight as a steel rod, due partly to never-forgotten lessons in deportment from a strict governess, but mainly to well-laced corsets. After lunch she had an hour's nap, then had another short walk. If the weather was inclement she spent most of the day at her needlework, except of course on Sundays, when she spent the time reading her Bible: that was the only acceptable reading matter on the Sabbath. On Sundays Miss Fox attended her local church for both the morning and evening services. She was "At Home" every Tuesday afternoon, but had very few callers.

For the duration of the bombardment, Miss Fox had sat stolidly in her drawing room, adamantly refusing to shelter in the basement with Mr and Mrs Barton, though she had insisted that Sarah take shelter with them. Sarah had wanted to go home to see if her children were safe, but Mrs Barton persuaded her that she would be in great danger on the streets and the boys would no doubt be quite safe in their own home, which was some way from the sea-front, and therefore not likely to be in the line of fire. This did not greatly alleviate Sarah's anxiety. There had been a few broken windows from blasts at the back of Miss Fox's house, which faced the sea, but fortunately there was no damage to any other part of the property.

Brian and Donald reminded Miss Fox of her brothers when they were young, and she was enjoying their company. "Mrs Hollis," she queried, "who looks after these boys when you are here?"

"I'm afraid they have to look after themselves, ma'am," replied Sarah. "But they are very capable," she added hastily. "They are at school most of the day. They're good boys," she added defensively.

"I'm sure they are," Miss Fox agreed, dryly, then after a slight pause, went on: "During their school holidays, you could perhaps bring them here with you." The more she thought of it the better she liked it, and she went on eagerly: "They could play in the garden on fine days, and during the bad weather...well, the nursery is still more or less as it was when my brothers and I were young. Would you like that, boys?"

Donald and Brian nodded enthusiastically, they liked the idea of exploring this great house with its large garden, what a wonderful place to play in.

This was a side of her employer that Sarah hadn't seen before. She thought the old lady was a martinet, always finding fault and complaining. Miss Fox suddenly looked younger, in fact being in her middle sixties she wasn't as old as her staff thought. It would appear that she was quite human after all.

"Aren't we going to Grandma's in Leeds then?" asked Donald.

50

The short mid-week service seemed to be going on longer than usual, and Mrs Morgan gestured irritably at Dulcie and Charlotte fidgeting in the pew as the vicar droned on about something or other. Neither of them paid any attention to what he was saying. After what seemed like several hours, but was in fact only ten minutes, Reverend Shaw concluded his sermon and announced the last hymn.

"Thank goodness for that," Dulcie whispered to her sister. "I thought he was going to go on all day. I want to see what's happening outside."

"I think it's stopped," Charlotte whispered back. "I haven't heard anything for a while now."

"Shh!" Mrs Morgan was becoming more and more annoyed with her daughters' behaviour this morning, especially Dulcie's.

Charlotte was correct, the bombardment had stopped a short while ago. During the singing of the last hymn the verger again made his way to the pulpit and had a brief conversation with the vicar. Before pronouncing the Benediction, Reverend Shaw informed his congregation that the German warships had left the harbour and it was now safe for them to leave the church. He raised his hands in an attitude of blessing and gravely intoned: "Lord, now lettest thou thy servants depart in peace, according to thy word. In the name of the Father, the Son and the Holy Ghost. Amen."

"Amen," the congregation dutifully repeated in unison. There was a brief silence, then a muted buzz of conversation as they hurried out of Church with unseemly haste, anxious to see what damage, if any, had been done to their properties. Dulcie and Charlotte were amongst the first out, in spite of their mother's futile attempts to restrain their unladylike exit.

"Gosh!" said Dulcie, as they saw the damage to the church and its surrounds. The top of the spire had been knocked off and the debris scattered in the churchyard; many buildings in the immediate area had been damaged. This usually elegant area of the town was a shambles. Even as they were standing there they could hear the strident insistent clanging of a bell, as an ambulance sped down the main road.

"Come girls, hurry, we are later than usual, you should be on your way to school by now."

"We're not going to school today, are we, mother?" Dulcie asked with genuine surprise.

"And why not, may I ask? The danger is past, the enemy ships have gone. Why shouldn't you go to school?" Mrs Morgan's tone dared them to argue, they followed her obediently and consoled themselves with the thought that at least there'd be something more exciting than usual to talk about today, with their school friends. Much to Charlotte's and Dulcie's disappointment, and to Mrs Morgan's relief, their own house showed no damage at all, not even a broken window. Several houses in the vicinity had been damaged to a greater or lesser degree. They were told by cook that Mrs Temple, an acquaintance of Mrs Morgan's, who lived on the opposite side of the road, had been killed and her husband injured. Mrs Morgan pointed out with irrefutable logic, that if the Temples had been regular churchgoers they would have been at the Wednesday morning service and therefore, would have been quite safe from attack.

"Huh," said Dulcie to her sister, "can you imagine if

everybody went to church in the middle of the week like we do, it would have been so full that the Germans could have just fired straight at the church and knocked it down and killed *everybody*." Charlotte nodded in agreement.

"Girls! I will *not* tell you again. It is time you were at school. Hurry yourselves."

"Yes, mother," they chorused dutifully in unison.

51

Jack Watson did not go straight home when he left hospital. Like Dora Stafford, he'd been advised to wait until the bombardment ceased and it was safe to leave. He walked straight down to the Foreshore, his few possessions wrapped in brown paper wedged under his arm. Jack was appalled by the devastation on all sides of him. Buildings were burning, most of the property along the sea-front was damaged, the road was littered with rubble and there was a large hole in the side of the lighthouse, which no longer had a dome atop. The familiar setting was unrecognisable. Ambulances were ferrying the injured to hospital, rescuers were carefully sifting through the damaged buildings looking for casualties. Cautiously stepping over the debris on the pavement, Jack went down the first slipway and walked along the sands by the water's edge. Turning his back on the havoc on the landward side he gazed out to sea for several minutes. He loved the sea in all its moods, but after today, he knew it was unlikely he'd ever feel the salt spray on his face again. There was a swell on the sea, which gave the illusion that the billowing waves were towering above him before they broke into white foam a few inches in front of Jack's toes. He'd known for some time that his days were numbered. The hospital staff and his own doctor had pretended optimism, but Jack was not fooled. The pains were more frequent and more intense, they were lasting much longer and the medication he was given was losing effect. He was fairly sure he would not see 1915, yet he had few regrets: life hadn't been easy, but he had enjoyed it on the whole. He was sorry to be leaving Gwendolen, his wife of nearly forty years, but he knew she would cope without him, they'd had many a long separation when he was at sea, and she'd proved to be a very capable woman. She'd brought up their family virtually on her own, and all were a credit to her. At the thought of Gwen, Jack gave a deep sigh and continued on his way, he had no doubts that his wife had safely survived the bombardment, but he wanted to see for himself that she was all right. He arrived at his little fisherman's cottage less than five minutes later: apart from a few cracked and broken windows there did not appear to be much damage in the street.

"Jack! I wasn't expecting you home," cried Gwen joyously, "they must think you're a lot better to let you come home."

"Aye," said Jack cheerfully, "have yer got t' kettle on then?"

As she bustled about preparing a massive breakfast for him, Gwen told Jack how she and several other neighbours had taken shelter under the wharf.

"By gum, it wasn't half cold! Half of 'em hadn't had time to get dressed and there they were in their nightclothes wi' coats ower t' top. They looked proper sights," she chuckled in amusement at the recent memory, then stopped abruptly as with tears in her eyes she told him sadly, of the death of little George, and of Raymond's severe injuries.

"Aye," Jack said again, as he contemplatively drew on his pipe. George had only had five short years, whereas he'd lived over sixty, and that was something to be thankful for. "Poor little buggers," he said quietly. The smoke from his pipe brought on a coughing fit that lasted several minutes.

He gathered the phlegm in his throat and spat on the fire. Gwen was hovering anxiously by the arm of his chair.

"Are you all right, love?" she asked fearfully as his breathing stabilised, "shall I go for Doctor MacPherson?"

"There's nowt he can do. Sit down, lass, I've summat to tell you," Jack said solemnly.

52

Nutty Slack was enjoying his third glass of beer with his brother Cyril. Plodder was quite happy in the field at the side of Cyril's house, enjoying an unexpected holiday. He'd recovered from his unaccustomed gallop and had calmed down. Cyril had welcomed Nutty warmly; the brothers did not get together very often. Cyril was only too pleased for a legitimate excuse to take time off work on his smallholding; he had two hefty sons, Adam and Timothy, to do most of the work for him anyway. The young men were both in their mid-thirties and neither showed any inclination to leave home and get married, they seemed quite content to take over the running of the smallholding. Cyril was quite happy to let them get on with it, he did very little himself these days. Cyril's wife Hilda was equally welcoming, and immediately made her brother-in-law a cup of tea and set a plate of fresh home-made scones in front of him. Cyril had thought the occasion called for something stronger, however, and produced a small keg of beer from the outhouse off the scullery, where it was keeping cool. So, in spite of the unfortunate circumstances that had brought about this unplanned meeting, the two old men were enjoying themselves. They ended up spending the entire day together; drinking beer, smoking their pipes companionably, doing justice to Hilda's wonderful cooking and baking, reminiscing about their boyhood and talking about the future. Nutty told Cyril about his plans to retire immediately.

"Me and Plodder's getting too old for this lark. Poor beast nearly killed hisself charging off like that this morning."

"Aye," replied Cyril reflectively, "I'm thinking of taking things a bit easier meself, letting t' lads do a bit more like." Hilda snorted derisively!

"If you take things any easier you'll spend t' rest of your life asleep!" she told him. "Not that anybody'd notice t' difference," she added reflectively.

53

Tony Kirk knocked on the back door of his friend's house. No-one ever went to the front door, which was used only for special occasions like weddings and funerals. At all other times it was bolted top and bottom and locked with a strong mortice lock.

"Is your Ronnie coming to school, Mrs Thornley?" asked Tony as the door was opened by a formidable-looking woman who glared fiercely at him.

"Ronald! *not* Ronnie, if you don't mind. Come in, he's getting ready."

"Is your *Ronald* coming to school, Mrs Thornley?" Tony amended as he followed her into the kitchen. He wiped his nose on the sleeve of his jacket.

"Give over, you mucky little tyke!" Mrs Thornley admonished sharply as she cuffed him across the back of his head. "Here, use this." She handed him a clean piece of rag torn from an old sheet, that was lying on the top of a laundry basket filled with newly ironed clothes. Ronald clattered down the linoleum-covered stairs which led straight into the kitchen.

"Me Mam said I have to go to school, Mrs Thornley, but me Grandad said it's a waste of time because our school's been bombed," Tony announced dramatically.

"Ooh, Mam, can't I stay home today?" Ronald looked hopeful.

"Rubbish! Yer going. Mrs Kirk knows it's all right or she wouldn't have sent Anthony." Mrs Thornley was a stickler for using the names on people's birth certificates, she despised shortened versions. Her own name was Gertrude; she would not answer to Gert or Gertie. Her husband was Victor, and nobody dared refer to him as Vic in her hearing.

Reluctantly, but resignedly, the boys set off with their arms entwined around each other's shoulders.

"Hey, you should have seen me Grandad!" Tony started laughing so much he couldn't continue with his tale immediately. "He went to t' lavvy and t' roof blew off. I thought it was because he'd farted too loud, but it was one of them shells from t' German boat. He didn't half swear!" He spluttered, helpless with mirth. Ronnie gave a hoot of laughter and the two boys clung together at the thought of old Mr Kirk with his trousers round his ankles and the roof suddenly opened to the sky.

At the time it had not been particularly funny. Mrs Kirk had been standing at her kitchen sink positioned just under the window, when she heard a terrific crash and saw the roof of the lavatory, at the end of the yard, blown off, along with that of her next-door neighbours.

"Father!" she screamed, but as she ran out into the backyard, she was soon satisfied he wasn't hurt when she heard the vehement language erupting from the damaged outhouse.

"It's right you know, t' school *has* been bombed, it's a waste of time us going," Tony was convinced. "Well, we'll just have to go home again then, won't we?" said Ronnie logically.

"Aye, but we could have had longer in bed."

The two nine-year-olds discussed what they would do with their unexpected holiday, so sure were they that there would be no school that day.

"Cor, look at that over yonder!" Tony interrupted Ronnie's detailed itinerary for their proposed day off; he pointed to their left. The cluster of back-to-back houses in the neighbourhood had been hit: some were quite badly damaged. They were so close together it had taken only an odd shell to create havoc. Fortunately, nearly all of the occupants had taken shelter in the Market Vaults otherwise the casualty list might have been high. Tony and Ronnie, temporarily rendered speechless, stood and watched as some of the men tried to effect some emergency repairs by boarding up broken windows, and their womenfolk searched for belongings and kitchen utensils that could be salvaged. Many of the women were crying, worried about their immediate prospects. Someone shouted to ask the boys what they were staring at. Embarrassed at having observed so much distress they hurriedly went on their way, temporarily subdued. With the seeming callousness of youth the boys almost immediately put the scenes they had just witnessed to the back of their minds and returned to discussing Tony's Grandad's predicament, which set them off laughing uproariously once more. Two women walking in the opposite direction looked at them disapprovingly, no one should be laughing after what had happened earlier in the morning, but several other people smiled at their merriment. Still laughing, they turned the corner, and the school came into full view. They stopped abruptly, bewildered, baffled and disappointed, their laugher suddenly silenced. The building looked exactly the same as it had done when they'd left it the previous afternoon. Children were making their way to assemble in the school playground and await the bell that called for them to line up and march into their respective classrooms. There weren't as many children as there usually were at this time of day though. Mr Duggleby, who taught both boys, drew level with them. "Sir," Tony stopped him, "Sir, we heard that t' school had been bombed, but it hasn't." His voice trailed off disconsolately.

"A school *has* been damaged, Kirk, but it was Gladstone Road School, not this one. Come along, you'll be late," and laughing at their obvious disappointment, Mr Duggleby hurried on into school. Unwillingly Tony and Ronnie followed their teacher into the playground and lined up with their classmates.

After the register had been called the whole school assembled in the hall for morning prayers. There were fewer children present this morning, they had much more room to spread about instead of being crowded in rows, shoulder to shoulder. There was a lot of shuffling of feet and whispering, but when the headmaster, Mr Fleming, strode in looking very grave, there was instant silence. Mr Fleming looked round the hall before clearing his throat, and in sepulchral tones broke the news of the tragic death of George Harrison, and the terrible injuries suffered by Raymond Turner. There was a shocked silence, then some of the younger children who were in the same class as the two little boys began to cry. The headmaster decided that the children were too distressed to continue with the normal morning assembly. After saying prayers for the bombardment victims, followed by a half-hearted rendering of "There's a friend for little children above the bright blue sky", Mr Fleming signalled to the teachers to take their individual classes out of the hall. All the children were very subdued, and not in the mood for lessons. However, their teachers were determined to try and proceed as normally as possible, even though they themselves were deeply shocked by what had happened. And so the school day took its course, although some of the very young infants were so distressed they had to be sent home during the morning.

54

She wouldn't openly admit it, but secretly, Ellie Armstrong was beginning to be worried about Joss. He was usually home long before this. She stole another surreptitious glance at the ornate clock on the mantelpiece, almost quarter to nine; he was never later than quarter past eight, and she was fearful he'd been caught in the bombardment.

The children were still underneath the table playing with Joshua's wooden Noah's Ark, each child had several pairs of toy animals and as they put them in the ark they made the appropriate animal noise. At times it became quite cacophonous, they'd been warned a few times by both Edie and Ellie to keep quiet. Now Edie said: "I think it's time we got these bairns to school, it looks as if the shelling has stopped. It's been quiet for about quarter of an hour now."

"Awww!" came a concerted wail from underneath the table. "We can't go to school today," said Joshua stubbornly.

"And why not?" asked Ellie sharply.

"Well, I expect the school's been bombed, so we might as well stay at home, anyroad we'll be late now."

"You won't know whether it's been bombed until you go and find out. They won't bother about you being late today. Anyroad you won't be late if you go now. Get your coats on and look sharp about it!" Edie said in a tone of voice that brooked no argument. The children, including Martin who hadn't yet started school, scrambled from under the table and quickly fetched their coats. Just then they heard the sound of the front door opening, Ellie gave a sigh of relief.

"You're late!" she said more sharply than she intended, as her husband came into the room; she had been more worried about him than she'd realised.

"Aye, I've been helping to dig a family out of a house down t' road, a woman and bairn killed and others badly hurt." Edie stifled a scream. The children looked frightened.

"Is it safe now?" she asked her brother-in-law. "We were just going to send t' bairns to school."

"Oh aye, t' German ships have gone now, but there's been some damage to t' school." Joshua glanced triumphantly at his mother, as the children gave a little cheer. "Yer still going!" Ellie told them. While they were still protesting they heard a sharp knock on the front door and the sound of it opening, a few seconds later Ted entered the already crowded room. The look on his face silenced everyone.

"What's up, Ted?" asked Joss. "What're you doing here so early?"

"It's Barney," said Ted brokenly, trying to keep back the tears. He told them what had happened. All the children simultaneously burst into tears. The dairy manager had arrived at Mrs Johnson's within ten minutes of being informed about the incident. He'd taken one look at Ted and ordered him home, then he'd made arrangements with the knacker's yard man for Barney's body to be disposed of.

"Shush shush, it could have been worse, it could have been any one of us," Ellie tried to comfort the children. "Aye, that's just what Mrs Johnson said," Ted sadly agreed. "I suppose it's summat to be thankful for."

Ellie busied herself making another pot of tea for the men; the five children crawled back under the table, still sobbing loudly. The two families sat down to mourn Barney, there was no more talk of school for the time being!

55

Clive and Daisy Weston, along with Jane Cattle, were still sitting in Charlie Jennings' domain, the basement of Gladstone Road School. The sound of the shelling had been so loud, it seemed to be directly overhead. Suddenly all the noise stopped, they sat listening for a few minutes, then Charlie stood up.

"Stay there. I'll go and see if it's safe for you to go out." The children did as they were bid and sat quietly, huddled close together. Charlie returned a few minutes later looking very sober. They looked at him anxiously

"Aye," he said heavily, "it's all over. They've gone - them bloody Germans have gone." He suddenly sounded angry. With some trepidation the children followed him out of the cellar, wondering what they would find. Children were filtering through the gate into the large playground in ones and twos and small groups, a few teachers had also arrived. They stood and looked at the ruins of their school, not knowing what to do, until the headmaster, Mr Grainger, arrived and took charge. The infants department was barely touched. The younger children were marshalled into lines, and taken into their part of the school by their teachers, under the supervision of headmistress Miss Golding. The older children, many of them in clothes inadequate for wintry weather, stood shivering in the schoolyard, waiting for a decision to be made. On closer inspection it was found the main hall had suffered the worst of the damage, and three classrooms were unusable for the time being. The children whose classrooms were intact were sent to them. The other pupils were dispersed amongst them, a few in each class. The overcrowding was not as bad as would have been expected because many children had not turned up for school that day. There were only a few days to the end of term, then they would break up for the Christmas holidays, so that the immediate difficulties wouldn't be for too long. The school holidays would give a breathing space to re-organise.

"Thank God this didn't happen half an hour later," said James Grainger to his staff, when the emergency teaching arrangements had been sorted out. There was a murmur of agreement: half an hour later the whole school would have been assembled in the hall and the casualty list would have been horrendous, it didn't bear thinking about.

56

"Mr Quinlan, are you there, Mr Quinlan?" Mrs Gregory rapped loudly on her neighbour's front door. Within a few minutes she heard a shuffling of feet and the sound of two bolts being drawn back, followed by a key being turned, before the door was finally opened. Mr Quinlan peered owlishly at her through his thick-lensed glasses.

"Why, Mrs Gregory, is something wrong? You're not injured in any way are you?"

"No, Mr Quinlan, it's my lodger. I can't get any reply from her room and the door is locked. I haven't heard the baby for a while, and I can usually hear her during the morning. It's over an hour since the attack finished. I haven't heard anything at all. I've knocked and knocked on the door and I've shouted. I'm worried something may be wrong." Mrs Gregory was getting more and more agitated. "Her rooms are at the back and I think that side of the house has been damaged, but I can't see from my windows," she concluded breathlessly.

"Don't upset yourself, dear lady, I'll come with you and see what I can do. But I'm afraid you may be correct about damage. Several of our rear windows are broken." With a shouted word of explanation to his wife, Mr Quinlan followed Mrs Gregory into her house. As she had said the door to her lodger's room was firmly locked.

"What is your lodger's name, Mrs Gregory?" queried Mr Quinlan. "Mrs Cameron - she's Scottish," was the whispered reply.

"Mrs Cameron, Mrs Cameron?" called Mr Quinlan, but there was only silence. No sounds at all emanated from the room. "I think, with your permission, dear lady, I had better try and force the door open. You haven't a spare key by any chance?" he added hopefully, as an afterthought. Mrs Gregory indicated that she hadn't another key, and waited anxiously while her neighbour went off to fetch a tool to force open the door. He returned much quicker than she could have expected followed by a young man.

"I met Keith outside, he'll help us." Keith Pickard was a joiner by trade, he had been passing Mrs Gregory's house, carrying his bag of tools on his way to a job, as Mr Quinlan had arrived at the front gate, and readily agreed to help. With the aid of a chisel and with the minimum of damage to the door he soon had the lock free, but he was still unable to open it. "It looks as if there's something blocking it," he observed, "is there a way round the back? I may be able to get in through the window."

"Yes, yes there is." Mrs Gregory wondered why she hadn't thought about it earlier. She showed Keith the way through to the back garden, and within a few minutes Mr Quinlan and Mrs Gregory heard the sound of something being moved from behind the closed door. Keith opened it and stood to one side. He'd had to move a large bookcase, which had fallen and blocked the exit.

An icy blast came from the room as soon as the door was opened, the large window which took up most of the outside wall had been blown in, the curtains flapping in the faint breeze made the only sound.

"They're in here," he said quietly, "but prepare yourselves for a shock." He paused. "I'm afraid they're both dead." Mrs Gregory gave a gasp and put her hand to her mouth. Fiona Cameron was sitting in an armchair with her baby in her arms; her right breast was bared as if she had been about to feed the child. Mr Quinlan looked away in embarrassment; he had never before seen a semi-naked female. In spite of being married for more than thirty years, Mr Quinlan had never seen his wife completely unclothed. Mrs Quinlan undressed and dressed under a voluminous nightdress. She removed her dress, put her nightdress over her head, without putting her arms in the sleeves then with a series of contortions removed her undergarments, then she thrust her arms into the sleeves. She reversed the process when getting dressed. They always made love in the dark under the bedclothes. Keith Pickard had no such inhibitions, he knew that the young woman and her baby were dead, but to make absolutely sure, he moved forward to take a closer look and confirm that was indeed the case. There was no doubt about it, but there were no marks on either body, they looked peaceful as if they were asleep.

"I think they must have died of shock." Keith had heard of this happening. "Perhaps we'd better send for a doctor," he continued.

Mrs Gregory nodded; she was too distressed to speak. She had become quite fond of Fiona Cameron in the few weeks since the young woman had become her lodger, and the baby, Heather, a little girl aged five months, was like the grandchild Amelia Gregory had never had. Fiona had told her landlady that she was a widow who had fallen on hard times, but Amelia was fairly certain that the young woman was unmarried, and had probably been turned out of her parents' home because of the shame she had brought on them. Mrs

Gregory, a staunch Christian, was not judgmental, and abiding by Christ's admonition: "He who is without sin cast the first stone", she accepted her lodger and her beautiful baby with open arms, and without question. Keith led Mrs Gregory and Mr Quinlan out of Fiona's room and into the large kitchen, he persuaded the old lady to sit down in her wooden rocking chair. He requested that Mr Quinlan make a pot of strong tea, while he himself went off to find a doctor. Feeling helpless by his neighbour's distress, Mr Quinlan put the kettle on, then scuttled back next door to fetch his wife, guiltily relieved to be out of the house.

57

"Well done, everyone, well done," congratulated headwaiter Peter Jones of the Grand Hotel. *"Tres bien, mes amis, merci beaucoup,"* echoed his *alter ego* Pierre, using up about half his French vocabulary in one go. Breakfast was over; the guests had not been inconvenienced at all by the damage to the hotel. The four members of staff who had prepared and served the meal were gathered in the debris-strewn dining room, surveying the scene with some dismay.

"Sorry, boys and girls, it has to be cleared up," Peter told them cheerfully. "But!" he paused, they looked at him expectantly, waiting for him to continue, "but, before we get on with it…" he paused again theatrically, as with a flourish he picked up the decanter of wine still standing like a crystal sentinel amid the shambles of glassware and crockery on the sideboard.

"See if you can find some glasses still whole, Jimmy," he said to Jimmy Dean, who disappeared into the pantry and found plenty of tumblers safe in a cupboard. Ceremoniously

Peter poured each of his colleagues a liberal measure of wine. The tumblers obviously held much more liquid than wine glasses, so the amounts were more than generous. When the decanter was empty, Peter threw it with dramatic force to the floor, where it smashed into hundreds of tiny pieces, unnoticeable amongst all the other shattered glass. "I've always wanted to do that," he said with some delight, as he raised his glass: "*Bon Chance!*" he said "Let's hope the buggers don't come back - we'll be ready for 'em if they do! By heck Jimmy, it's a good job you got up a bit earlier this morning, you'd have missed all this." He gestured with his wine glass. Everyone laughed, including Jimmy, clearly relieved that there had been no casualties in the hotel. After that everyone felt quite merry and they happily set to work sweeping up the broken glass and clearing up to the best of their ability.

58

Ben Winter, Maurice Atkinson and Andy Nelson, had arrived at Mr Ulliott's grocery store.

"I'm not going in there, the old bugger'll kill me," said Andy apprehensively.

"Of course he won't. Anyway, we'll come in and explain to him," said Ben. "Nothing was your fault lad, he'll understand," he said reassuringly.

"He won't," muttered Andy, not at all convinced. "He'll kill me!" he repeated.

The three young men entered the shop. As soon as he saw Ben and Maurice, Mr Ulliott came forward immediately, ready to be of service. He caught sight of Andy cowering behind them.

"Where have you been?" he asked harshly. "Get that next

delivery out straight away," he went on, without waiting for a reply. "Now gentlemen…" he turned obsequiously to Ben and Maurice. His manner changed when he was told what had happened to the cartload of goods. Mr Ulliott was furious. As Andy had predicted his boss blamed him for it.

"I suppose it's my fault the bloody Germans bombarded us," he countered. In spite of Ben's intervention, supported by Maurice, Mr Ulliott continued to berate his errand boy, and finally told him he was sacked.

"Oh no, he's not, he's resigning," said Ben formally. "I'll be obliged if you'll pay what's owing to him up to date."

"Pay him what's owing? Pay him what's owing? There's nothing owing to him. He owes me for the loss of a delivery cart and various goods," Mr Ulliott blustered. Maurice pulled a business card from his waistcoat pocket.

"I am a solicitor," he said, conveniently forgetting to mention that he was in fact, merely a trainee. "I am representing this young man. We will call back later today. Please have his wages ready. Withholding them could be construed as stealing." He paused. "I expect you have insurance to cover your losses." With great dignity he gave a short bow, turned and walked out of the shop, closely followed by an amused Ben and a flabbergasted Andy.

"I hope he doesn't call your bluff," said Ben to his friend. "Now young fellow," he turned to Andy, "instead of being an errand lad, how would you like to be a messenger boy? I have a vacancy for one in my office." This wasn't strictly true, but once Ben had told his father the whole story, he was sure a position could be found for Andy, especially as with so many young men going off to war, there would be plenty of vacancies shortly. The former errand lad was speechless, all he could do was nod his head.

59

There had been no lack of volunteers to help dig out victims buried under collapsed buildings. Under the guidance of the professionals, unemployed men, retired men, young boys and those who just happened to be passing to or from work, gave their services. It was a slow, painstaking task; they had to be very careful, moving bricks cautiously, so as not to dislodge more rubble on to the people they were trying to rescue.

Frank Porter, Bob West and the other men had moved to a new location, after recovering Anne Ellis's body from the ruins of the Co-op. They were attempting to find any victims that might be buried under the two adjoining houses at the end of a terrace.

"Hello, love," said Frank as they cleared away the remains of the kitchen roof of the end house, and exposed the angry face of a woman streaked with dust. "Are you all right? Not injured are you?"

"Go away!" she screeched at them, "go away, leave me alone."

"Nay lass, we've come to get you out. Why, it's Enid Mason isn't it?" as he recognised her.

"*Miss* Mason to you, Frank Porter. Go away!" she said again. Frank laughed, they'd been at school together and he was blowed if he was going to start calling her "Miss Mason" after all these years.

"Don't be silly, Enid lass, are you injured?" he asked again, as the men carefully continued to remove debris from around her. Enid and her mother had been buried for almost four hours by the time the rescuers got to them. Enid suspected her arm was broken, it was so painful, as was her shoulder, and she had a bump on her head the size of an egg, where a falling brick had hit her and knocked her out, giving her a raging headache. Before the house had collapsed she had already had three cups of tea, and inevitably was unable to control her overfull bladder. She felt ashamed and embarrassed, and preferred to suffer the pain of her injuries rather than let these men know that she had wet herself, especially when one of them was Frank Porter, who used to tease her unmercifully when they were at school together more than twenty years ago.

"Where's Mother? is she dead?" Enid asked fearfully. Her emotions were mixed, she'd often wished her mother dead, but now that there was a real possibility that she might have been killed, Enid felt afraid and guilty that her wish might have been granted.

"We're still digging, love, don't worry, we'll find her," someone, she didn't know who, called. "Let's get you out first."

"Go away, leave me alone," Enid repeated heatedly through clenched teeth. "Find mother."

"You can't stay forever, woman," Frank retorted, losing patience with such stubbornness.

"Well, she's obviously OK, leave her for the time being, let's try and find the old lady," Bob West intervened impatiently; the others agreed and set to work looking for Mrs Mason and any other victims that might be under the ruins of the house next door.

Miraculously, Mrs Mason had suffered only a few cuts and bruises, her big bed had fallen through the ceiling and somehow got wedged in such a way that it gave her protection from the rest of the falling masonry above. The old lady was carried to an ambulance that was standing by, in spite of her protests that she was all right and didn't need treatment. This was in complete contrast to her usual complaining about every little ache and pain.

"Where's our Enid? Is she dead?" she queried.

"She's OK, Missus, but she won't let us pull her out," called one of the rescue party.

"Oh well, leave her then." Mrs Mason tried to push away the nurse from the ambulance, who was attempting to ascertain the old lady's injuries. "Get off, I'm all right."

"I can tell that you are," said Nurse Harper dryly. "I'll go and see what I can do for your daughter."

With a great deal of discomfiture, Enid whispered to the nurse why she didn't want the men to help her out of the rubble. "Oh, is that all?" commented Nurse Harper brusquely, "don't worry about it." She went and took a thick blanket from the ambulance and called the men to remove the rest of the debris. The nurse wrapped the blanket around Enid's wet skirt and stockings, immobilised her injured arm, then ordered two men to carry her to the ambulance, being careful not to jolt her injured arm. If any of the rescue party knew what had happened, they didn't let on, but Enid blushed profusely as she was carried to the ambulance, her embarrassment greater than her pain.

60

"You'll have to go back to your own ward, Mr Benson, it's not visiting time you know." Christopher Benson gazed uncomprehendingly at Staff Nurse Barbara Walters. He had been sitting silently by the bedside of his unconscious father for over two hours, hardly moving, unable to take in what had happened earlier that morning. He did not feel the pain of his own injuries, he was too numb for that.

"Come along, Mr Benson, I have work to do." Nurse Walters was becoming impatient at the lack of response.

"Nurse!" A sharp voice behind her made her jump. "Nurse, a word, if you please," said Matron. Barbara followed Miss

Richardson to the nurse's desk at the end of the ward with some apprehension, wondering what she'd done wrong.

"Yes Matron?" she asked respectfully.

"Do you know that young man has just been bereaved?"

"Yes Matron," Barbara replied, puzzled by the question.

"Then why were you speaking to him like that? Why were you ordering him to leave his father's bedside? Don't you feel he needs a little compassion?"

"Yes Matron, but it's not visiting hours and I … "

"Nurse, nurse," Matron interrupted her impatiently, "*I* know the rules, but in some situations rules must be bent. This poor young man has lost three members of his family this morning, and I fear his father will not recover. He's not in anyone's way is he? he's not disrupting the ward is he?"

"No, Matron," Barbara agreed. "Then leave him to have this time with his father." Miss Richardson paused. "It won't be for too long," she added sadly. She realised the young nurse was being over-zealous, interpreting the rules rather assiduously. Barbara looked rather shame-faced as she said: "Yes Matron," and at a nod from Miss Richardson went back to her duties, leaving Chris to his vigil.

61

Sergeant John Somerford of the King's Own Yorkshire Light Infantry, waiting at York railway station for the train to take him to Scarborough, noticed much activity at the end of the platform. A battalion of troops was being paraded, standing smartly to attention with their rifles sloped on their shoulders. John idly wondered where they were going. He didn't have to wait long to find out. When the train arrived the first two carriages had reserved signs on all the windows. The soldiers boarded the train in an orderly fashion, filling the two carriages to capacity. There were not very many other passengers to fill the rest of the carriages and John easily found himself a corner seat, put his kitbag on the luggage rack and settled down for the one-hour journey. Almost as soon as the train pulled out of York, John dozed off, he opened his eyes briefly when the train stopped at Malton; no passengers alighted or boarded the train, which was quickly on its way again. When the train stopped at the small village station of Seamer, John woke properly, knowing he was nearing the end of his journey. He looked out of the window as familiar scenes came into view and the train pulled up in Scarborough station. The soldiers filed through a gate, normally used for freight, specially opened up for them at one end of the platform. The rest of the passengers queued to hand their tickets to Billy Bowman, who was still on duty, feeling absolutely fed up and wishing the day would come to an end. He noted the troops going through the goods entrance at the far end of the station.

"Bloody typical, that is, turning up after it's all over, bloody typical," he said belligerently to no one in particular: some of the passengers thinking he was talking to them looked annoyed, others were puzzled, they didn't know what he was talking about. The news of the bombardment had not yet spread generally, very few of the public from outside the town boundaries knew about it yet.

By tomorrow everyone who could read a newspaper would know.

John looked round eagerly, hoping to see Anne; she wasn't there but his brother Michael was waiting. The brothers shook hands and embraced briefly. Excited at being home after so long, John didn't notice Michael's lack of enthusiasm at his brother's homecoming.

"How are you, Mike? It's good to see you. How's everyone? Where's Anne? I thought she might be here to meet me. It is her half day isn't it?"

John's questions came in rapid succession, giving no time for Michael to answer. John stopped abruptly as he noticed his brother's expression. "What's wrong? Has something happened?" They were outside the station by now, and for the first time John took note of the surroundings. Several buildings in the vicinity were damaged, with parts of roofs missing, and windows cracked or broken.

"Bloody Hell. What's happened?" John asked with a sharp intake of breath.

The soldiers from the train were standing to attention in the station forecourt and at a barked command from their Company Sergeant Major, executed a rapid, smart right turn and at a second command marched away in the general direction of the sea.

"What's happened?" John asked again quietly. Michael told him of the bombardment that had been endured during the morning.

"It lasted less than half an hour, but there's a hell of a lot of damage. There were lots of people injured, and some killed. They're still digging 'em out so there'll mebbe be more." Michael hesitated. With a sense of foreboding, John knew there was more to come. "Go on," he prompted.

"It's Anne, there's no easy way to tell you. She and Stella were buried when part of the Co-op building was shelled." Michael stopped and swallowed hard. John waited, not saying anything. Controlling his emotions, Michael continued.

"Stella was very badly injured. She'll probably lose her leg." John became impatient: "And Anne? What about Anne?"

"Anne … Anne was … Anne is … " Michael couldn't continue, he turned his face away and blinked away his tears.

"She's dead, isn't she?" said John tonelessly. His brother nodded dumbly, without turning his head.

"Let's go home," said John in that same flat voice. He was too numb to think. Why should this have happened to them? They'd had so much to look forward to after their long separation.

62

It took the rescue workers several hours to clear enough debris to uncover the occupants of the house next door to the Mason's.

"This is where Renee Page lives," Bob West informed them. There was a brief derisive laugh from the gang of men. Irene had quite a reputation in the district. Something pink showed through the rubble.

"I think we've found her," said Frank Porter gravely; the laughter was forgotten as the men redoubled their efforts to release Irene. They soon realised that she was not alone, a man, half dressed, was lying beside her. Both were dead.

"Wonder who he is," one of the men commented. "One of her fancy men, I expect," someone else replied, "poor bugger."

"Hang on!" Cec Lindhurst, a middle-aged man, a joiner by trade who had been helping with the rescues all day, recognised something about the portly corpse.

"Hang on, I think it's Wedderburn."

"Wedderburn the chemist?" Frank Porter sounded quite incredulous. "Bloody Hell, Cec, you're right. What was he doing at Irene's?" The men guffawed and some crude reasons were suggested. The joking was a way to give them relief and to ease the tension they'd been under all day. The sights they'd seen had sickened them: they were depressed by the dead bodies they'd dug out of ruined buildings, and horrified by some of the injuries they'd encountered. Their laughter had no mirth in it, and was in no way meant to be disrespectful to the victims. They had been moved to tears on several occasions by the scenes they'd come across that day. The laughter quickly died away, and they carried on with the grisly task of removing the latest casualties of the bombardment from the remains of Irene's house.

63

Emily Wedderburn had gone back to her own house within a few minutes of the last shell being fired. The Brayshaws had found it hard work trying to converse with her. They had tried to be pleasant and chatty, but their efforts had met with only monosyllabic replies, while the two little girls, Phoebe and Sophia, gazing disconcertingly at their unwilling hosts, didn't say a word the whole time they were in the cellar. The Brayshaws had soon given up, and for most of the time they sat in silence. They were as relieved as Emily when the shelling ceased and she announced she thought it was safe to go home. She thanked her neighbours politely, they made no attempt to dissuade her, and followed by her pale daughters she went back to the only place she felt comfortable, her own house. The house was empty, as she'd expected: she assumed that Herbert would be busy in his chemist shop by now. Emily busied herself preparing breakfast for herself and the girls, she hurried them up a little as breakfast was later than usual, then sent them off to school, as she could see no reason to keep them at home now the danger was past. From then on she followed the usual routine of the day, assuming her husband was doing likewise.

64

There was some confusion in the normally orderly routine at the Court House. Harold Yeomans, the epitome of punctuality, had not turned up. Apparently the telephone wires had been damaged, as frequent attempts to call him had resulted only in a dead line, and finally a messenger had been sent to Mr Yeomans' house in the Crescent. Alfie Ingleby watched with interest as the messenger returned red-faced and breathless.

"That fella's out of condition, he needs more exercise. Probably spends all day sitting on his fat arse pushing a pen." He sniggered at his own wit.

"Shut up, Alfie!" PC Hardcastle admonished him wearily. The constable was in no mood for flippancy from Alfie or anyone else, he'd already had an extremely traumatic day and his shift was only half over. Well, at least he wouldn't be too long in Court; apart from Alfie - and his was a straightforward case, he'd been caught red-handed - there were only a couple of drunks and a woman accused of stealing a cabbage from a market stall to be dealt with that morning. The woman's defence was that she'd picked the cabbage up when it rolled off the stall, and was going to put it back. She was unable to explain why she still had it under her coat when she left the market.

Instead of each defendant being called individually, as was the normal procedure, the Clerk of the Court summoned everyone to enter the courtroom. This was very unusual, to say the least. They wondered what was happening. Everyone remained standing while Mr Gregory White and Mr Hubert Jackson, the presiding magistrates entered and stood in front of two of the three large chairs on the bench. The third chair remained empty. Mr White cleared his throat and gazed sternly about the Court room.

"It is with deep regret I have to announce the sudden death

of our esteemed and worthy colleague, Mr Harold Yeomans."
There was a gasp of consternation, then a confused murmuring
from the body of the Court.

"Quiet in Court!" called the usher sharply. Mr White gave
him a baleful look, as the noise subsided, then solemnly
announced:

"Mr Yeomans died as the result of a German shell, which
damaged his home this morning. There will now be a two
minutes' silence," he ordered.   Court officials, defendants
and their representatives, obediently stood with bowed head
for two minutes that seemed much longer. The silence wasn't
absolute, there was some shuffling of feet, clearing of throats
and coughing. Although they wouldn't dare admit it out loud,
some of the accused were rather relieved that Mr Yeomans
wouldn't be presiding on the bench that morning. He had a
reputation for being very severe in his sentencing for even the
most minor crimes.

"Now!" said Gregory White abruptly, making everyone
jump, "let's get on with the morning's business. Mr Pollard
has been sent for to take Mr Yeoman's place. He should be
here very soon; we won't wait for him. Call the first case,"
he instructed the clerk, who had ushered all the defendants
out into the waiting room again.

"I'm sick 'o this, marching in and out," said Ada Palmer,
the woman accused of stealing the cabbage. "I can't be
hanging round here all day, you know, I've to get home to get
me old man's dinner ready."

"What're you giving him, Ada? Boiled cabbage?" called
out one of the waiting men. Everyone laughed, Ada looked
offended at first, then she too joined in the laughter. The
clerk of the court frantically tried to quieten the defendants;
he was the only one in the room who did not find the remark
at all amusing.

Alfie's case didn't take long; he had no defence, having being caught with the goods about his person. Because everything could be returned to its rightful owner his sentence was perhaps not as severe as it might have been. He was sent to prison for eighteen months.

"Ah well, Mr Hardcastle," he said philosophically to Derek as he was being taken downstairs to the cells to await the prison van, "at least I'll have somewhere to sleep in this cold weather and a decent Christmas dinner!" He laughed merrily. PC Hardcastle made no comment.

65

The loud authoritative knocking at the front door startled Emily Wedderburn, who was in the middle of making a steak and kidney pie for Herbert's dinner. Quickly wiping the flour from her hands with a tea towel, she had almost reached the door when the knocking re-commenced.

"I'm coming, I'm coming," Emily muttered as she unlocked and opened the door, to find a policeman standing on the step. She stared at him, waiting for him to speak.

"Mrs Wedderburn?" Bernie Maynard hated breaking bad news, he'd done it many times before, but it wasn't something one ever got used to. It was an unpleasant and regrettable task that had to be carried out, and today in particular it was one that had needed to be done several times over.

The woman who confronted him was young; he thought she would have been pretty if it were not for her severe hair style, which made her look older that her years, and the stern, unwelcoming expression on her face, as she waited for him to speak.

"May I come in, Mrs Wedderburn, I'm afraid I have some bad new for you."

Without speaking, Emily stood ungraciously to one side, Bernie removed his helmet as he entered the house. Somewhat reluctantly Emily showed him into the comfortless unheated front room.

"Would you like to sit down, Mrs Wedderburn? It would be better if you did."

"No, just tell me what you've come to say," she replied stiffly. Bernie cleared his throat, then as gently as he could told Emily about the rescue workers finding her husband's body, though he was careful not to specify where.

"Is the shop badly damaged?" asked Emily.

"The shop? Er, I don't know, what shop?" Bernie was taken aback, it wasn't the reaction he had expected.

"Well, he left here to go to his shop, he has a chemist shop. If he's been killed because of being buried under a pile of bricks, then the shop must be damaged. How bad is it?"

"Er.. Well actually, he wasn't found in his shop, he ... er ... he went to help a neighbour and was caught in the house when the shell hit it," Bernie explained with tactful diplomacy.

"He was caught all right. Some woman's house I suppose. And I bet I guess whose. " Emily sniffed. "Thank you for informing me, constable, " she said formally, "now if you will excuse me I have arrangements to make. I suppose Herbert's been taken to the Mortuary?" Bernie nodded speechlessly; he'd had many reactions to news of bereavement but never one like this. Shock affected different people in different ways, he told himself, nevertheless, this was one that he had never encountered before. He thought Mrs Wedderburn's reaction was very strange to say the least.

"We would like you or a relative to formally identify the ... er ... body, at your convenience? Would you like me to inform anyone, a relative, a friend, or a neighbour perhaps, to come and be with you?" he finished lamely.

"No, thank you, I'll come myself later," said Emily

dismissively. "Good day, constable." There was nothing Bernie could do but leave. She almost shut the door in his face, and there was a thin smile playing about Emily's lips, as she made her way back to the kitchen. An air of confidence she had never shown before replaced her usual nervous demeanour. It was as if her husband's sudden death had released her from fetters. All her life she had been subservient to men, first her strict father then her imperious husband, but not any more, no, never again. "I am a woman of property," she said aloud. "I am free and independent. A rich widow."

She gave a little skip as she went towards the table to finish making her steak and kidney pie, before setting out to make her "arrangements."

Sophia and Phoebe did not come home from school during the day, they took sandwiches and the family had their main meal during the evening when Herbert arrived home, but of course he wouldn't be home today or any other day, thought Emily. Leaving the prepared pie on the kitchen table, covered with a clean white cloth, Emily washed her hands, took off her apron, put on her coat and hat and went out. Her first call was to the shop: she was relieved to find it was completely unscathed, not even a cracked window. She was surprised, however, to find it open for business. Norman Soames, Herbert's dispenser, had his own key to the shop. He was very annoyed that Herbert had not turned up to open the shop, especially on this particular morning. There were more customers than usual clamouring for attention, due to minor injuries received during the bombardment. It wasn't his job to serve customers, his duty was to dispense prescriptions and occasionally to give advice to customers with minor ailments who couldn't afford to visit a doctor.

"Mrs Wedderburn!" Norman exclaimed in surprise when Emily walked in, she very rarely visited the shop, as Herbert did not encourage it. "Mrs Wedderburn, where is your husband? I am rushed off my feet." To the great interest of the customers in the shop, Emily stiffly informed him of his employer's sudden death.

"We'll arrange to employ an assistant for you, Mr Soames, until then you'll just have to manage." There was a buzz of conversation as she left, her attitude had shocked most of the listeners; Emily did not give the impression that she was a grieving widow. Having satisfied herself that her inheritance was intact, she went along to see Mr Browne, the nearest undertaker, where she quickly made arrangements for the funeral, before going on to the mortuary, where she unemotionally identified her dead husband. She asked for no details about how or where he was found, and none were volunteered. With her arrangements satisfactorily concluded, Emily then went to break the news to Herbert's sister, Beatrice Harding.

"Herbert's been killed during the bombardment. I've made the arrangements. The funeral will be on Saturday at ten o'clock. You'll tell the rest of the family, won't you? I'll see you on Saturday then," she informed her sister-in-law in short staccato sentences, then she left abruptly, leaving Beatrice, shocked and upset, unable to take in the news at first. She was dumbfounded by her sister-in-law's apparent change of personality.

"The bitch," she said of her sister-in-law, whom she'd never really liked. Emily had an air of superiority in spite of her timidity. "The cold-hearted bitch," her anger momentarily superseded her shock and grief. Quickly putting on her coat, Beatrice ran to the hardware shop where her husband was manager. By the time she reached the shop she was sobbing wildly.

"The bitch, the bitch," she kept repeating, "she's after the shop. Well, she's not going to get it!" she said fiercely. "That was my father's shop, it's not hers."

Arthur Harding was fitting a piece of board over a broken window, as a temporary measure until the glass could be replaced; he was relieved to find there was not too much damage to his shop. He saw his wife running down the street, she ran into his arms sobbing wildly.

"It's our Herbert, he's been killed!" she cried. "That bitch of a wife of his has just been round. She's not a bit bothered, she doesn't care, she's just after my father's shop," she sobbed incoherently. Arthur tried to calm his wife, her wild grief was mixed with fury at her sister-in-law's callous attitude and she wouldn't be comforted.

66

"There's a policeman here to see you, Miss Thompkinson." Julia Thompkinson glanced at the clock on her desk as her secretary stood uncertainly in the doorway. It was nearly ten minutes to four, only a few minutes until the end of the school day.

"Did he say why he's here, Clare? You'd better ask him to come in," the headmistress went on without waiting for an answer. Julia Thompkinson was an attractive-looking woman in her late forties. She had been headmistress of St Agnes' School for girls, for almost ten years - irreverently and inevitably, known as "Aggies" by its pupils. Ahead of her time in her thinking, she believed that education was as important for girls as it was for boys. Fortunately she had had understanding parents who were proud of their daughter's achievements. She had won scholarship after scholarship and eventually, after a lot of hard work and hours of intense studying, and opposition from male colleagues, she had secured a Master's degree in History. Even so her father thought that perhaps it was a waste of time and money as surely she would marry, give up everything, and settle down to be a dutiful wife. Julia, however, had no room for marriage in her plans; she had turned down two proposals to concentrate on a career. Her suitors had felt relieved rather than rejected; they found her intellect very intimidating. Julia firmly believed in women's suffrage, but did not concur with the followers of Mrs Pankhurst that violence was the way to win. She didn't think that running into the path of fast-moving horses, chaining oneself to railings or throwing bricks through the windows of public buildings were ways to achieve the right to vote. Julia had been on several peaceful demonstrations: along with other women graduates she had marched in procession in her academic gown through the streets of several large cities, London, Manchester, Newcastle amongst others. This was to emphasise the fact that exceptionally intelligent women were not allowed a say in the running of their country, while a man of the lowest mentality, could put his cross on a voting form without even understanding why. Her teaching methods were considered rather *avant garde* by some people, but no one could deny the results were impressive. Several girls, emulating their headmistress, had gone on to university and obtained good degrees. True, most had later married, but a few had persisted with their careers.

The young policeman entering her office was at first overawed by the sight of the efficient, handsome woman, smartly dressed in a crisp white blouse and black skirt, her hair neatly coiled in plaits around her head. It reminded him of his own schooldays, not too long ago. He was soon put at ease by an encouraging smile.

"Good afternoon, constable. What can I do for you?" Julia realised that he was nervous and understood the reason. He looked very young, hardly older than some of her pupils. "I must be getting old," she thought, amused.

The policeman cleared his throat: "Miss Thompkinson? Miss Julia Thompkinson?" he asked even though he knew who she was. She smiled again, and waited to hear what he had to say.

"Er ... I'm afraid I have some bad news. I'm sorry." Julia surreptitiously glanced at the clock as PC Jonathan Barlow paused. He cleared his throat again and continued hesitantly.

"Er.. we've had a telegraph message, from the North Riding Constabulary. Scarborough was bombarded from the sea by German warships this morning." Julia gave a start, and gave the constable her full attention. Her only brother lived in Scarborough.

"Geoffrey?" she whispered almost inaudibly. PC Barlow did not hear her and continued:

"We have been informed that your brother, Mr Geoffrey Thompkinson, is missing." His message was delivered in a formal monotone, as if he was reciting a memorised directive. "I'm sorry," he added with more emotion, then stood helplessly waiting for Miss Thompkinson's reaction. After a brief silence, in which Julia absorbed what she had been told, she courteously dismissed Jonathan Barlow: "Thank you, constable, thank you for telling me. Not a pleasant duty for you, I know." With a smart salute the young policeman left, relieved that the headmistress had not had hysterics as he'd half-expected before he met her. He now knew she was the sort of woman who would efficiently take everything in her stride.

For a few minutes after PC Barlow left her office, Julia sat with her elbows on the desk and her hands covering her face, then giving herself a little shake she rang the small hand bell on her desk, and her secretary came in immediately. Julia glanced at the clock: it was four o'clock, the end of the school day. Even as she thought it the school bell clanged out, releasing the pupils from their classrooms.

"Clare, I've had some disturbing news, and I'm afraid I must go to Scarborough immediately. Would you ask Miss Daniels to come and see me now, please?" As Clare left her office Julia picked up the telephone and asked the operator to connect her to Sir Harvey Clifton, the chairman of the school governors.

"Julia!" Sir Harvey's loud voice blasted in her ear, "How lovely to hear from you. How are you, my dear?" The chairman was half in love with the headmistress and made no attempt to disguise his feelings; a constant source of amusement, not only to Julia but also to the rest of the board of governors and the school staff as well. Quickly, Julia explained about the message she'd received and her intention of leaving for Scarborough immediately. "Which means, of course that, regrettably, I will not be here for the last couple of days of term."

"Of course my dear, of course. Don't worry about a thing, we'll manage, your staff are very efficient and well-trained," Sir Harvey boomed, almost deafening her with his hearty voice. "Let me know if there's anything I can do, won't you, my dear?"

As Julia replaced the receiver Cynthia Daniels, the timid Deputy Head, poked her head round the door of the office looking worried, as usual. Once again, Julia explained about the message she had received, and of her plans to go to the East coast straightaway. She had been planning to go the following week after the end of term, to spend Christmas with her brother and sister-in-law.

"So, I'm afraid you'll have to supervise the end of term activities, Miss Daniels," Julia concluded, Miss Daniels looked terrified at the idea. "Clare will help you with the administration." With that she dismissed her nervous deputy, who scuttled away like a frightened rabbit. She gave the minimum of instructions to her competent secretary and hurried home to pack a few things, then caught the next train across the Pennines.

67

In the depressing, uncomfortable waiting room at the hospital, three people sat in silence on the hard upright wooden chairs, staring into space. Mr and Mrs Reynolds, Stella's parents, had been told only that their daughter was in the operating theatre. They knew no details of her condition, except that her leg had been crushed and she had head injuries. Not knowing was adding to their anxiety.

Joe Turner had every faith in the surgeons who were treating Raymond. He had already accepted that the boy would be crippled for life, but anything was better than that his son should die. Joe loved all his children, even though he didn't often show it. He sat on the edge of his seat clutching his cloth cap in his hand.

The three occupants looked up expectantly, as the door to the waiting room opened. Sister Cecilia entered, she smiled encouragingly at Mr and Mrs Reynolds, but it was to Joe that she turned.

"Would you like to come with me, Mr Turner. You may see Raymond now," she told him gently. On the way to the ward she tried to prepare him for Raymond's condition, which was still critical.

"He's not out of the wood yet, Mr Turner, not by any means, but we are hopeful. We shall all pray for him."

To Joe Turner nuns were rather mysterious women who lived behind closed doors, only venturing out occasionally. He was rather intimidated by being in such close proximity to one and could only nod dumbly. Raymond was in a bed in the corner of the ward with screens around it. He looked as if he was sleeping peacefully. The doctor standing by the bed nodded briefly to Joe.

"I'm sorry, we've had to amputate his right foot above the ankle," he said in a tone of voice that conveyed no sorrow at all. "He has a few other injuries, but they are insignificant by comparison. Good day to you," and with that the doctor abruptly left. Joe was not unduly upset by the doctor's tone; he was overawed by authority, and was used to being addressed in such a manner. With a serene but heartening smile, Sister Cecilia indicated the chair by the bedside and when Joe was seated she left him alone with his little boy. He sat patiently waiting for Raymond to regain consciousness after the anaesthetic.

~

Cissie Wellings glanced at the big wall clock in the hospital foyer, only a few minutes, then she could go to the ward and visit her brother. She had been told that Sam Benson was still unconscious and that Christopher was by his bedside, but had been given no further information on her brother's condition. Her red-rimmed eyes and white face bore evidence that earlier that day she had wept copiously over the bodies of her sister-in-law and her two younger nephews. How she wished Duggie were here, but her husband was at sea and not expected to arrive home for another two days. The strict hospital rules regarding visiting hours were never challenged, and she waited impatiently for the large pointer of the clock to approach the hour. At three minutes to two, Cissie went upstairs to the ward. She was the first visitor through the doors and a nurse showed her where to find her brother. Like Raymond in the ward on the floor below, Sam was in a corner bed with screens round it. She was not warned of what to expect, and the blood drained from her face and she put her hand against the wall to steady herself, as she felt suddenly dizzy at her first sight of her brother and nephew. Sam was barely recognisable, his face was swollen and bruised, and his hands lying on top of the counterpane were heavily bandaged. Chris, sitting on a chair by his father's bedside, did not look at her, he did not seem aware of her arrival. His lacklustre eyes were firmly fixed on Sam's face. Cissie sat down abruptly in a chair on the other side of the bed from Chris, she did not know what to say and Chris did not seem to be aware of her presence. She sat silently, tears streaming down her cheeks, and wondered how much more grief she could cope with. She had no illusions after seeing Sam; she had very little hope that he would survive.

68

As he made his way home with his brother Michael's arm sympathetically resting on his shoulder, John Somerford was appalled at the devastation all around him. It was already dusk, and the lamplighter was on his way round lighting the gas lamps, which softened the surroundings to a grey ghostly hue that partly concealed the injury done to the town centre. John felt full of anger and grief that such a violent and unprovoked occurrence had deprived him of his fiancée. It did not take the brothers long to reach their parents' house. Their father was in the kitchen on his own, looking pale and shocked.

"Hello son," he said as they briefly embraced, "what a home-coming for you. They let me off work early to be here to welcome you. What a home-coming," he said again, "what a welcome." He shook his head. "Your Mam's at Mrs Ellis's, she's been there since we heard." He broke off, his voice choked with emotion. He looked at John's bleak face but didn't know any words of comfort; he turned away so his sons wouldn't see the tears in his eyes.

"I'll go round … I'll go round and see them," John said huskily. "Yes, I'll go round now."

"I'll come with you," said Michael. John looked at him gratefully, he gently patted his father's shaking shoulders. "I'll see you soon, Dad," and the brothers left the house.

69

Although visiting hours were from two until four o'clock in the afternoon and six until seven o'clock in the evening on Wednesday and Sunday only, Matron had relaxed the rules for some of the relatives of the bombardment victims. It was late evening before Mr and Mrs Reynolds were able to see Stella. She lay in the narrow hospital bed, so pale and still that at first sight her parents thought she was dead. A few minutes later her eyes fluttered open, but she seemed unaware of her surroundings.

"Stella, can you hear me? How are you feeling love?" asked her mother. Gradually Stella focused on her mother's face.

"Hallo, mum," she said weakly, "I don't know how I feel. What happened? Have I had an accident?" She grimaced with a sudden pain. "My leg hurts."

"Which one, dear?" asked her father with some trepidation. Stella pointed vaguely in the direction of her right leg, and her parents exchanged a troubled glance. The limb was no longer there, it had been so badly crushed the surgeon had amputated it. The decision as to whether or not to tell her at that moment was taken out of their hands, as Stella lapsed into unconsciousness again. A nurse appeared as if from nowhere.

"I think you had better go home now, she's not likely to be fully conscious for some time yet. Come back tomorrow." The Reynolds meekly did as they were told and left the ward.

"At least she's alive," whispered May Reynolds to her husband, "I don't know how I'm going to face Carrie Ellis." Her husband merely nodded as he took her arm and led her out of the hospital.

70

As the light faded, the gangs of men who had been sifting through the damaged buildings decided to call it a day. They were satisfied that there were no more people buried. They were tired emotionally and physically. None of them had ever encountered the scenes they had experienced today. The injuries of many of the victims were horrific, and the rescuers had been shocked, saddened and very angry by the sight of the mutilated bodies of little children.

"Right lads," said Bob West wearily, "I think that's about all we can do for today. See you tomorrow." Murmuring their "goodnights" the men went their separate ways in a subdued mood. The following day and many days after would be spent clearing away debris, repairing buildings that could be repaired, and demolishing those that couldn't .

71

Sally Foster watched the visitors leave the hospital, the end of the visiting hour indicated that her shift would soon be at an end. It had been a long busy day, Sally was tired but she felt a glow of satisfaction. She felt that today she had done some real nursing as opposed to skivvying. As she made her way to the nurses' cloakroom, Matron came towards her with the two nuns.

"Thank you so much for all your help," Miss Richardson was saying as the trio arrived at the main door, "we've appreciated your hard work. Please thank your Mother Superior for allowing you to come."

"It has been a pleasure," replied Sister Frances, sounding as if she meant it, while Sister Cecilia smiled in acquiescence. "If you should need our help tomorrow, please do not hesitate to contact Mother Superior. Goodbye." Both nuns inclined their heads in farewell, they glided down the hospital driveway, then crossed the road at the corner and disappeared into the convent. Sally put her hand over her mouth to stifle a giggle. The movement of the nuns' wimples had reminded her of the fluttering of birds' wings. Matron glanced sharply at her but her mouth twitched suspiciously and there was a twinkle in her eye as she said: "I think it's time you went off duty, Nurse Foster. You worked very well today. Thank you."

Sally didn't know what to say, she blushed in embarrassment at the rare words of praise, then simply said: "Thank you, Matron," gave a little bob of a curtsey and went to collect her outdoor garments. Miss Richardson sighed as she went to do another round of the hospital. It would be another couple of hours before she left the building, after being on duty for almost thirteen hours. She wouldn't go until she was satisfied that her patients were as comfortable as possible for the night.

72

It was quite late when Julia Thompkinson reached her destination, almost ten o'clock. Fortunately there were still several cabs plying for hire in the station, this was the penultimate train of the day. Julia did not register the debris around her; the effects of the bombardment were muted by the soft glow from the gas lamps. The cabby encouraged his horse to move at a swift trot and they reached her brother's house within ten minutes. A strange young woman, who introduced herself as Ruth Jenkins, opened the front door almost immediately. Before they went into the living room, Ruth explained what she and her employer had seen from the house on the cliff.

"Richard called the police immediately, and a boat was launched to search the area. They haven't found anything yet," she said lamely. "I'm sorry," she finished sympathetically, her tone indicating that there was not much hope of finding Geoffrey alive.

"Mrs Thompkinson is naturally very distressed, so I thought it was better if I stayed with her."

"Thank you, thank you, I'm very grateful for all you have done," said Julia sincerely. She paused. "Tell me honestly, Miss Jenkins, is it likely that Geoffrey may be found alive?" Ruth hesitated only momentarily. "No, Miss Thompkinson, I don't want to give you false hope. I don't think there's any chance of your brother being found alive, and although I hate to say so, you must face the possibility that his body may not even be found." Julia merely nodded, it was what she had feared, and she knew it was going to be difficult, if not impossible, to convince her brother's wife that she must face the unpleasant fact that she was now a widow. She braced herself for the meeting with her sister-in-law.

Followed by Ruth, Julia went into the living room. Audrey

was huddled in an armchair, she burst into tears as soon as she saw her sister-in-law: "Julia, I'm so glad you've come," she said pathetically. Julia moved towards her and put her arms comfortingly round Audrey's shaking shoulders. Jasper, his head resting on his outstretched front paws, looked up and slowly thumped his tail twice, but did not come running to greet her as he usually did. He dropped his head down on to his paws again and just gazed sadly at her. "Jasper knows he's not going to see Geoffrey again," Julia thought sadly.

"Geoffrey's been gone all day, I'm so worried about him," Audrey wailed. Julia exchanged glances with Ruth, who whispered: "She still thinks he's just gone for a walk, she won't accept that there's very little chance of him coming home again. After what we saw, I can't pretend that he may have survived. I'm sorry."

"I know," sighed Julia, "but I'm afraid my sister-in-law is not very good at facing up to things." She sighed again.

"If you'll excuse me, I think I should be going. My employer will be wondering what's keeping me. Although I was able to send him a message earlier." Ruth had written a note and stopped a passing errand boy, and asked him to deliver it to Richard, with a promise of a reward on safe delivery. The boy had agreed with alacrity, the big house on the cliff wasn't too far out of his way, and Mr Lovell had a reputation for generosity. Even so, he was pleasantly surprised when instead of the penny or tuppence he was expecting, he received a sixpenny piece.

"Oh, Miss Jenkins, please forgive me, we have imposed on you long enough. I really am extremely grateful for everything you've done for us." Julia was apologetic at having presumed upon Miss Jenkins' good nature.

"I'll call in tomorrow to see if there's any news, if I may," said Ruth, with a smile as she took her leave.

73

Thursday December 17th dawned as grey as its predecessor, mirroring the mood of the majority of the town's population. There was a prevailing air of shock, incredulity and wonder that such a catastrophe could have happened to a normally quiet sedate resort. Many people who did not normally bother to read a newspaper made a point of buying one that morning. The headlines of all the national dailies proclaimed the devastation wrought not only on Scarborough, but also on Whitby and Hartlepool, increasing the sense of outrage. The Daily Mirror called it "The Wanton War on Women and Children", The Daily Sketch stated that: "German 'Kultur' means shells on Churches." The local paper, The Scarborough Pictorial, had damning headlines which took up half of the front page: "Scarboro' under fire", "Merciless Descent of Death and Destruction", "Defenceless Town Sacrificed to German 'Kultur' ". The first Lord of the Admiralty, Winston Churchill, referred to the attackers as "baby killers". In the town's entire history there had never been so much notice from the media and those in high office. The King himself sent a message of sympathy and support to the Mayor. However, all the attention provided no comfort to the bereaved.

74

Sam Benson died in the early hours of the morning. He briefly regained consciousness, and touching Christopher's hand he said: "Don't take on so, lad, it'll be all right," then, looking at a point somewhere behind Chris he said: "I'm coming, love." Chris glanced behind him to see who was there, but he could see no one. Nurse Phyllis Griffiths, making a routine check on her patients, caught a brief flash of light out of the corner of her eye, as she approached Mr Benson's bed. She assumed it must have been something from outside, as it wasn't repeated. Chris was still sitting by his father, as he had been all day. Phyllis automatically felt for Sam's pulse, but as she had expected, there was none.

"I'm sorry, Christopher," she said quietly, "I'm afraid he's gone." Chris nodded briefly as if in confirmation. "I think it might be best if you went to your own bed and tried to get a little sleep," she continued persuasively. Again Christopher nodded and allowed the nurse to escort him to the next ward. He hadn't spoken since he arrived at the hospital, and until that moment he had steadfastly refused to leave his father's bedside. But he knew that his vigil was now over. Despite swallowing a sedative, Chris didn't sleep; he spent the night staring into space.

75

Connie and Jim Harland spent a sleepless night, lying side by side in the big double bed, not talking. Laura and Suzie, bewildered and distressed by what had happened, had finally cried themselves to sleep, huddled together in the back bedroom. At intervals, Connie shook with sobs and Jim put his arm around her, but neither could find any word of comfort to give each other. Three times Connie got out of bed and went into Gordon's little room. She did not bother lighting a candle, she could see him lying on the narrow bed, his body softly lit by the glow of the gas lamp outside. She had refused to have his face covered. Connie tried to pretend that her boy was only sleeping, but knew she was deluding herself.

Jim did not go with her, each time she left the bedroom he lit another cigarette, and stared bleakly at the uncurtained window opposite the bed. He was not normally a heavy smoker, but in the hours since he'd heard about his son's death he'd lost count of the number of cigarettes he'd gone through.

76

John Somerford also spent most of the night smoking one cigarette after another. He'd gone to bed soon after midnight, he was weary after his long journey and felt drained after the emotional upheaval of the day. After lying sleepless, thinking of Anne and their wedding day which was now to be Anne's funeral day, he quietly got up, careful not to disturb his brother in the other bed. Downstairs he lit an oil lamp, which was set in the middle of the table, then he poked the banked-up fire and added more coal. John felt helpless, he hadn't known what to say to Anne's parents, and they hadn't known what to say to him. He was wishing the leave that he'd been looking forward to for so long was over, he wanted to get back on active service. He felt angry, he wanted to get his revenge on the enemy for what they had done to him, to Anne and to his home town. John picked up the kettle and was about to place it on the fire.

"I think we could both do with summat a bit stronger than that, lad." The quiet voice behind him startled him, so that he nearly dropped the kettle. He hadn't heard his father come into the kitchen.

"I couldn't sleep either," said Arthur Somerford, as he took a bottle of whisky out of the sideboard. "I got this specially for t' … well." He broke off.

"For the wedding," John finished for him. "Aye, well and

for Christmas as well mebbe." Arthur paused. "It's not going to be much of a Christmas," he said bleakly.

He poured two generous measures of whisky and the two men made an attempt to drown their sorrows in the strong spirit. They sat silently in the comfortable kitchen, each with his own thoughts, until John's mother came in at half past seven to prepare breakfast.

77

Stan Merriman had also found a modicum of comfort in the whisky bottle. When Seth and Henry had left him after the visit to the undertaker's parlour, Stan had set about cleaning up the shop. He worked like a demon, replacing merchandise on the shelves and clearing up the goods he had thrown about in his first burst of anger. He was still angry as he started clearing up the damage that the shells had wrought; furiously he threw broken glass and bricks into sacks. A few customers came by but were repelled by his irate cry of: "We're not open!" He didn't give any explanation and nobody dared ask him why: they quietly crept away, intimidated and very offended by Stan's attitude, until the news of Dolly's death leaked out, then they understood. Some went back to offer condolences, and help in clearing up, but were told in no uncertain terms to go away, or were ignored completely. It was quite late when all the debris had been cleared away, the shop tidied and the windows temporarily boarded up. Stan took one of the few bottles of whisky still intact, from the display shelf in the shop and went upstairs to the living quarters. He drank the whole bottle neat, then fell into a drunken sleep. It was eight o'clock the following morning when he woke. His mouth was dry, his head ached, and he was shivering; the fire had gone out during the night, the ashes lay grey and cold in the grate, making the room look bleak and cheerless. It took Stan a few minutes to realise why he was in such a state, then he remembered the events of the previous day. He put his head in his hands and cried weakly.

"Go away," he said when he heard a tentative knock on the outside door; he wiped his eyes with his sleeve, then when the knock came again slightly louder, he got unsteadily to his feet and went downstairs to open it.

"I am sorry if I'm disturbing you," said the young man on the doorstep, "I just called to see how you were. I don't want to intrude, I just wanted to know if you're all right." Stan thought he recognised the speaker but his head was whirling so much he couldn't think clearly. "I came yesterday to tell you ... er ... I came yesterday with Seth Adams. Henry Pike's the name. I say, you look pretty rough, can I do anything to help? Make you a cup of tea or something?"

"Aye," said Stan wearily, "come on up."

As soon as they were in the living quarters, Henry made Stan sit down, while he busied himself making a pot of tea, cleaning the grate and lighting the fire which was soon burning brightly, gradually the room began to warm up and to look more cheerful. Not so Stan, he sat with his head in his hands, oblivious of Henry's ministrations. He became aware that the young man had placed a large mug of strong tea on the side of the hearth within his reach. Henry was telling him something. At first he didn't understand the words, then it permeated his haziness that Henry was telling him he'd been with Dolly when she died. "I thought she was saying 'stand', like, and that she wanted to stand up, then Seth told me your name is 'Stan' and I realised that was what she was staying. 'Stan' not 'Stand'. The last word she said was your name," he finished lamely as Stan stared hard at him. "I ... er ... I hope that is perhaps a bit of comfort to you."

"Is that right? Is it?" asked Stan, with more animation than he'd shown up to then. Henry nodded. "I hope that's some comfort to you," he said again.

"Aye lad, it is," Stan replied wonderingly. "I don't know why but somehow … I don't know." He couldn't go on, his shoulders began to shake, and the tears rolled down his cheeks again. Henry stayed a little while longer, not caring that he would be late for work for the second consecutive day. When Stan calmed down and assured Henry he would be all right on his own, and in fact would like some time to himself, the young man took his leave.

78

Julia had persuaded her sister-in law to go to bed about midnight. She'd given Audrey a mild sleeping draught, a preparation that she took regularly for "her nerves", she'd told Julia. It took only a few minutes for Audrey to fall asleep, Julia made herself some cocoa, then took it into the living room; she lay back in an armchair and waited. She dozed fitfully through the night, jerking awake at every slight sound, wondering if someone was coming to give her news of Geoffrey, but no one came during the long night. Julia knew in her heart that Geoffrey was dead, he couldn't possibly have survived the fall from the cliffs to the rocks, and subsequent immersion in the sea. Nevertheless, she needed to have it confirmed, to see his body. Until she did, there would always be a very faint desperate hope at the back of her mind.

Audrey disturbed her at eight o'clock, she wandered in wearing her flannelette nightdress, looking abstracted and confused; she was shivering.

"Is Geoffrey back?" she asked pathetically. Julia shook her head, then putting her arm round Audrey's shoulders she guided her to a chair. She poked up the fire into a good blaze and added some more coal.

"Sit there, dear, I'll make some fresh tea and get you some breakfast. What would you like?" She tried to sound cheerful but her words had a muted desperation that sounded brittle even to her own ears. Audrey did not reply, it was as if she hadn't heard. Julia made the tea anyway and also some toast, which her sister-in-law accepted but did not eat, although to Julia's relief she did drink the tea.

"Tea, why do we always make tea in a crisis?" thought Julia. "I wonder how many cups have been made since yesterday. Is it because it calms one down or is it just something to do, I wonder?"

A light knocking at the front door interrupted her wandering thoughts. Jasper gave a little woof. It was Ruth. "I hope I haven't called too early, have you had any news?" she said as she bent to stroke Jasper, who had gone to meet her as if she was an old friend.

"It's so kind of you to come, no, it is not too early and no, I'm afraid there has been no news at all. I must look a mess, I didn't go to bed." The usually calm and controlled Julia felt flustered. "I've just made some more tea, that's all I seem to have done since I arrived. Would you like a cup?" Ruth nodded her acceptance. "My employer, Mr Lovell, has telephoned the police and the coastguard, and although more searches will be made I'm afraid we can only wait, to see if your brother's body is washed up." Julia could only nod dumbly, she didn't need to be told. Audrey sipped her tea, oblivious of the whispered conversation of the two young women. "Richard, Mr Lovell that is, sends his condolences and asked me to tell you that if there is anything he can do for you, do not hesitate to ask."

"Thank you," replied Julia, "you have already been so kind and we are strangers to you."

"Well, you see, Richard saw exactly what happened through his telescope, he feels sort of involved." Another knocking at the door disturbed their conversation. Jasper gave a low bark. It was a policeman.

"Have you found him?" asked Julia; at the same time Audrey called: "Is that you, Geoffrey?" She appeared at the door, still clad only in her nightdress.

"Please go back and sit down again, dear" Julia requested, and Ruth gently took Audrey by the shoulders and led her back into the living room. "Come and sit down by the fire and keep warm, Mrs Thompkinson."

"I'm sorry there is no news, miss," the policeman was saying to Julia, "I've brought you this, it was found halfway down the cliff caught on a small projection of rock." He handed her Jasper's lead. "I'm sorry," he said again. "We'll let you know as soon as we know something ourselves."

Julia thanked him as she shut the door behind him, she stood with her back to it, clutching the lead, for several minutes before she went back into the sitting room. For the first time since she'd heard that Geoffrey was missing, she wept. Jasper lay down with his head on his outstretched paws and whined softly.

79

In the middle of a sleepless night it suddenly occurred to Beatrice Harding that her sister-in-law had given her no details about Herbert's funeral. Apart from the fact that it was due to take place on Saturday, no place had been mentioned. She didn't want to waken her husband, as he had to go to work in a few hours, but she had a feeling of resentment that he could sleep in such circumstances. Eventually, just before six o'clock, Beattie could bear it no longer, and she woke Arthur.

"Arthur, Emily didn't tell us when Herbert's funeral is." Arthur yawned.

"Aye, she did lass," he said sleepily, "it's on Saturday. Ten o'clock."

"Yes, but *where* on Saturday? She never said *where*. I'm can't go round to ask her, I don't want ever to speak to her again."

"Well, we'll just have to find out for ourselves then, won't we? Leave it to me, lass. I might as well get up now. It's too late to go back to sleep."

"I'm sorry, Arthur, but I was that worried and angry."

" 'S 'alright, love, you stay there and I'll bring you a cup of tea in bed." Arthur yawned again and quickly dressed. Later in the day, true to his word, he found out all the details of Herbert's funeral. It wasn't a difficult task. There were not so many undertakers in the area and his plan was to simply make enquiries at those nearest to Emily's house. He struck lucky first time: Arthur knew Mr Browne slightly, so it was to him he went on his initial call, and was obligingly given all the details of the forthcoming funeral and an invitation to view the body beforehand. His task accomplished, Arthur conveyed the news to his wife and informed the rest of the family, knowing that Emily would not make any effort to do so.

80

In contrast to the majority of the other inhabitants of the stricken town, Emily Wedderburn had slept very well, she had the big double bed to herself and she revelled in it as she stretched out. She had gone to sleep thinking what she would do with the business, now that she owned it, and how she would spend the extra money she would possess, when Herbert's affairs had been settled. She hadn't yet decided whether she would keep the shop or sell it, but there was plenty of time to think about that. Her daughters had taken the news of their father's death with a quiet acceptance. Emily didn't know whether they were upset or not, she was insensitive to their moods. She loved them in her own way, but was not particularly interested in them. They hadn't seen a great deal of their father when he was alive; it was unlikely that they would miss him now he was dead. He'd spent long hours at work during the day, usually leaving before they rose, and often went out during the evening, not returning home until after they were in bed. He'd hardly noticed their existence. Sophia and Phoebe were happy enough in each other's company, and not knowing any better, they assumed all parents were like Emily and Herbert.

81

"By heck, Ted, I never expected you to come in today." Neville Earnshaw, manager of the dairy, was genuinely surprised when Ted Cox turned up at his usual time to start his milk round. "I thought you'd have a couple of days off at least. I was just loading up, I was going to do your round mesen'." He pushed his cap to the back of his brow and scratched the front of his head, a regular habit of his.

"Aye, well there were nowt to do at home, I'll be better off working than sitting brooding about poor old Barney. Have you a spare hoss for me then?" Ted asked unenthusiastically. He wondered how he was going to cope with a new horse after working with Barney for so many years. He had known of course, that he wouldn't be working with Barney for ever, the old horse would have been retired in two or three years' time. It was the sudden cruel way that Barney had been taken from him that had devastated Ted so much.

"I think you'll get on well enough with Betsy, she's very docile; you'll not have any bother with her," said Neville as he led the way to the stable, where a grey mare stared dispassionately at them. Ted stroked her, led her out to the yard and harnessed her to his already loaded milk-cart. With a brief wave to the manager he guided Betsy out of the yard to start his round. Ted's deliveries took much longer than usual, partly because Betsy was unfamiliar with the route, but mainly because so many people came to offer their condolences; Barney had been a beloved institution. When he finally finished work and returned to the depot, Neville was waiting for him.

"You're late back today, Ted, how did it go?"

OK, Nev, OK, I miss old Barney, I always will, but I think Betsy'll do. She'll soon get used to it. I think we're going to be friends, aren't we old girl," he said as he stroked the mare's nose, and offered some sugar lumps; she responded by nuzzling his neck, and snorting gently.

82

Mrs Mason and her daughter Enid had spent a restless night sharing the uncomfortable double bed. They were in the cramped top back bedroom with its sloping ceiling, in the house belonging to Mrs Mason's eldest son Roger and his snooty wife Marianne. She had been christened Mary Anne, but she thought that sounded too common for her current social existence. Her mother-in-law took perverse pleasure in calling her Mary Anne at every opportunity, to Marianne's fury. "She's no better than any of us," Mrs Mason was fond of saying, "so who's she to give herself airs and fancy names?"

"Do keep still, mother," pleaded Enid, gritting her teeth, "every time you move, you hurt my arm and my shoulder, and I've got a very bad headache."

"Well, how do you think I feel then?" Enid wished she hadn't spoken as her mother started on a long list of complaints, including bemoaning the loss of all her medicine. They had been treated at the hospital. Enid's arm was indeed broken, and her shoulder was badly bruised, but both she and her mother had been very lucky indeed to escape with such minor injuries. However, their house was uninhabitable, and they had only the clothes they were wearing; these were stained and covered in brick dust. They had no other choice but to avail themselves of Roger's and Marianne's grudging hospitality. Marianne had reluctantly gone out and bought a set of clothes and a nightdress each for her unexpected and unwelcome guests. They were not what the recipients would have chosen for themselves, but they had no choice but to accept them, ungraciously.

"I reckon she's got these from a rummage sale," complained Mrs Mason. "Where on earth has she dug this up from?" as she held up a blouse in a sickly green colour, that would in no way enhance either Enid's or her mother's complexions. Marianne carefully kept a record of exactly how much she had spent; she expected repayment in full as soon as her mother-in-law and sister-in-law were in a position to do so. "And I hope that's not going to be too long," she informed her husband. "It is most inconvenient to have them here, especially at this time of year. You don't suppose they'll be here all over Christmas, do you?" Marianne was horrified at the thought.

"I don't expect their house can be rebuilt in a week, dear," Roger replied mildly, "there's still a lot of clearing up to do before they can think of repairing."

"Perhaps they could go and stay with Hugh or Vernon," said Marianne hopefully, but knowing it was unlikely. Hugh, the second of Mrs Mason's sons, lived in Lincoln, and her youngest, Vernon, was a country parson in a small village somewhere in Buckinghamshire. "Well maybe later, dear, let's leave things as they are for now, eh?" Roger wasn't happy with the situation either, but he could hardly turn his sister and mother onto the streets.

"Well at least Enid will be able to help me with the heavier work." Marianne brightened up at the thought of having an unpaid servant.

"And if she thinks I'm going to be skivvying for her, she's got another think coming," Enid informed her mother, as she carefully got out of bed, shivering in the chilly atmosphere. "My God, it's like Iceland in this bedroom. My arm's too bad for me to be doing any housework, or any other kind of work. Anyway, I'm sick of waiting on other people."

"Meaning me, I suppose," said Mrs Mason indignantly. Enid just snorted, then gave a yelp of pain as she moved too quickly and jarred her injured shoulder.

83

"Goodness gracious me! What's up with you? Have you wet t' bed or summat?" Mrs Appleby pretended amazement as Iris came into the kitchen, fully dressed, before she'd even been called.

"No," she tried to sound casual. "No, I just wanted to be in good time for school." She was embarrassed by her mother's remarks, and only succeeded in sounding annoyed. Mrs Appleby smiled as she placed a steaming bowl of porridge on the table and poured a generous helping of thick cream over it.

"Here, get that down you. They won't be coming again today, you know," she added quietly, then more briskly: "Matt's gone to get a newspaper, t' postman says it's in all t' papers about us being bombarded." She sounded almost proud that the attack on Scarborough was the main news item of the day.

84

More children turned up at Gladstone Road school, than had attended the previous day. Mr Grainger and his staff had to find space for the extra pupils whose classrooms had been damaged. Miss Golding, head of the infants, offered a corner of the department's assembly hall, which was gratefully accepted by Mr Grainger, but not by the pupils who were sent there. They didn't want to go back to the infants, it was degrading, but there was no other choice, so they had to make the best of it. The head teachers of two other board schools within walking distance offered to take a few pupils and thus help to alleviate the situation, which was soon resolved satisfactorily, with a minimum of overcrowding in the classrooms that had remained intact. Term ended in less than a week, so the present position wouldn't have to last very long, and hopefully, most of the repairs would have been carried out before the beginning of the next term early in the New Year.

Brian and Donald Hollis returned to school after the events of the previous day. Admiring fellow pupils at break time and again during the lunch hour surrounded them, as they recounted their adventures. They told their appreciative audience of how they had been in direct firing line of the enemy warships, and how they had dodged the shells. How they had saved Andy's life by pulling him away from the path of the runaway tram in the nick of time. Finally how the rich old lady who was their mother's employer had been so impressed by their bravery that she had wanted to adopt them and make them her heirs. With every telling they added more embellishments to their tales, and their schoolfellows listened open-mouthed, never doubting the veracity of the narrative. Brian's and Donald's exploits somewhat eclipsed Clive, Daisy, and Jane being allowed into Charlie Jennings' boiler room on the previous day. They were now relegated to mere listeners instead of being the centre of attention.

85

Mechanically, Connie Harland prepared breakfast for her husband and two little girls. The atmosphere in the little kitchen was very subdued, nobody spoke. Both Connie and Jim were pale-faced and red-eyed, visible evidence of the sleepless night they had both had. Today the undertaker would call and put Gordon in his coffin, tomorrow he would be buried in the local cemetery. "And yesterday," thought Connie, "yesterday at this time he was so full of life, so excited about having his name in the paper." Was it really only twenty-four hours ago? It seemed such a long time since she'd opened the door to Constable Hardcastle. At the thought Connie suddenly burst into tears, causing Laura and Suzie to follow her example. Jim sat at the head of the table and was unable to comfort his wife and daughters; he was in need of comfort himself.

86

Stella had hovered between consciousness and unconsciousness all night: her condition was still very critical, but it looked as if she would live. She was still unaware that her leg had been amputated, or that her best friend was dead. These particulars would be withheld until it was felt she was strong enough to accept them. By that time Anne's funeral would already have taken place.

Little Raymond had slept most of the night, occasionally crying in his sleep as the pain penetrated his sedated state. The night sister had kept a watchful eye on him, checking his condition every few minutes. She was optimistic that in spite of his injuries the little boy would survive, and felt a glow of satisfaction.

Matron Richardson was back on duty by eight o'clock, heartened by the news about Stella and Raymond, but saddened, though not surprised, to hear that Mr Benson had died.

"He was too badly injured, and didn't have the will to fight, knowing he'd lost his wife and children," she sighed as she turned to her ward sister. "And what about Christopher?"

"Well Matron, physically he's not too bad, but he still hasn't spoken or shown any emotion, even when his father passed away." She consulted her notes unnecessarily. "He's still in extreme shock, and I've no idea how long that could last." Matron nodded. "I wonder if he would be better off being discharged," she said thoughtfully. "It may be that being in familiar surroundings could help him. When his aunt, Mrs Wellings comes, ask her about the possibility of taking him home with her."

Cissie Wellings was only too pleased to take her nephew home. She needed someone to look after; she needed something extra to do, to help alleviate her grief. Even though she had known her brother had little chance of surviving, his death had still come as a shock. Uncomplaining and obediently, Chris did everything he was told to do, like a child. With the aid of a pair of wooden crutches borrowed from the hospital, he haltingly made progress to the hospital foyer where he waited quietly, not moving until Cissie found a hansom cab - an unprecedented but necessary expense - to take them to her home, where she could fuss over him. Christopher showed no emotion or awareness at all, when his aunt led him into her living room and helped him to a comfortable armchair by the side of the fire. All the time she talked to him, "How would you like a nice cup of tea, love? What shall we have for dinner? Your uncle will be home from sea tomorrow, won't that be nice?" No reaction. "And what a homecoming," thought Cissie as she bustled about the kitchen, putting on the kettle, making the tea, then starting to prepare a meal for herself and Chris. She had to keep busy to stop herself from thinking too much, and all the time her nephew sat and stared into the fire, his face completely devoid of expression.

87

Walter "Nutty" Slack, with Plodder pulling the cart as usual, left the coal yard at his normal time to start his daily round. He'd enjoyed his unexpected day off the previous day. He and his brother Cyril had downed many pints of home-made beer - they lost count after the first half dozen - and had spent many hours chatting about the past, reminiscing about when they were boys, and the mischief they'd got up to. They tended to exaggerate and embellish their stories beyond recognition of the truth. Hilda, who had known them all their lives, had to correct their versions many times. Fortunately Plodder knew his way home, Nutty was too drunk to do more than hold on to the reins and leave it to the horse. He had quite a hangover this morning, but had forgotten his plans for immediate retirement. Tommy Collins was just coming out of his front door as the coal cart drew level. "Hey up, Nutty," he greeted, hoping the coalman would make no reference to losing his load of coal yesterday. Nutty ignored him. "You're not getting any more coal from me, yer bugger," he muttered under his breath. "No-body in this street's getting any more coal from me. They all had their share yesterday for nowt." He was appalled at the number of damaged buildings on his round, it had been too dark, and he had been too inebriated, to notice anything on his way home the previous night. Several of his regular customers were not there, having had to find alternative accommodation until their properties were repaired or in some cases wholly rebuilt. There were gangs of men all over town, making some buildings safe and demolishing others.

"Bloody hell, Plodder," Nutty said to his horse, "our Cyril's lucky living where he does, he knows nowt about all this." He paused. "If you hadn't bolted, we'd have been in the thick of it all. You might even have saved our lives, and we both had a good day in t' end didn't we?" He chuckled at the memory of the relaxing convivial day he'd spent with Cyril and Hilda. He had returned home with a basketful of his sister-in-law's home-made cakes and scones, and an invitation to spend Christmas Day at the smallholding the following week.

88

"You knock," Emma Jones told her friend and neighbour Maggie Hammond. "No you, you're nearer than me," was Maggie's excuse. They were standing close together so the difference in distance from Daniel Hudson's door was minimal. The two women had been round the immediate locality with a shopping basket, collecting money towards little Georgie Harrison's funeral. Although the majority of people in the area didn't have much themselves, they gave what they could, a ha'penny here, a penny there, occasionally as much as twopence from a few households, but not very often, few could afford as much as that. They had left Daniel's house until the very last, deterred by his reputation, and now as they debated who was to knock and ask for a donation, the door suddenly opened, startling them both.

"Well?" growled Daniel as he blew a cloud of cigarette smoke into their faces, "what do you gossiping biddies want?"

"Er, hallo, er Mr Hudson," stammered Emma, ignoring his rudeness, "we … er … we … "

"Get on with it!" Daniel said impatiently, "I haven't time to stand here all day. What do you want?" he asked again. Maggie took her courage in both hands.

"We're collecting for little Georgie Harrison's funeral and we wondered if you would like to give something," she said in a rush, without pausing for breath.

"Well, why didn't you say so in t' first place 'stead of farting about?" Daniel disappeared into his cottage, leaving the two women standing uncertainly on the doorstep. He was absent for several minutes; Maggie and Emma began to wonder if he was coming back and whether they should just quietly leave, when Daniel reappeared and thrust something into Emma's hand. Giving a sort of growl, Daniel firmly shut the door in their faces. The two women looked incredulously at what Daniel had given, unable to believe the evidence of their own eyes.

"It's a sovereign," whispered Emma, "a *gold sovereign*," she repeated, her voice rising. Maggie gave a low whistle through her teeth: "By heck, you don't see many of them round here. In fact you don't see *any* round here. Well, we can't call him an old skinflint any more can we?" she said.

"No, but he's still a cantankerous old bugger, however generous he is," was Emma's reply. They laughed as they left Oxley's Yard, and went back to Emma's little cottage on Quay Street, where they could count the money collected. They emptied the contents of the basket onto the kitchen table and sorted it into piles of farthings, halfpennies and pennies, with the occasional threepenny bit, and the sovereign. When they finished counting it, they found they had collected more than two guineas, thanks to the unexpectedly generous contribution from old Daniel.

"By heck, I never thought we'd get that much," said Emma. "Come on, let's take it round straight away. Here, we'll put it in this." She took an old tin tea caddy from the shelf, "and Florrie can keep the tin as a present," she added. Emma tipped the money into the caddy. "By heck, it's heavy," Maggie remarked as she picked it up. They made their way round to the Harrison's. They could easily have taken a few coppers for themselves, no one would have known, but the thought never entered the mind of either of them. Poor they might be but they prided themselves on being honest. The door of the Harrison's house was opened by a little girl of about eight years old, with a snotty nose; her shabby cotton dress was inadequate for the chill of the December day. She stared at them with red-rimmed eyes, and sniffed.

"Is yer Mam in, love?" asked Maggie. The child turned and shouted into the room behind her: "Hey Mam, it's Mrs Jones and Mrs Hammond."

"Hello, Florrie love," said Emma, when Mrs Harrison came to the doorstep, "how are yer, love?" Without waiting for an answer she went on to explain about their collection for Georgie's funeral. Florrie Harrison was touched at her neighbours' generosity: it was no secret that the family would be hard-pushed to find enough money for an unexpected funeral. She was dumbfounded when told of the amount contributed by Daniel Hudson.

"Well, I never, who'd have thought an old skinflint like him'd give owt. Did you hear that, Will? Old Hudson's given a gold sovereign for our Georgie?" She turned back to her two neighbours without waiting for an answer from her husband. "Do you want to see our Georgie, he looks right bonny." It was obvious Florrie would have been very upset if Emma and Maggie had refused to see Georgie. She was unnaturally calm, and there was no sign of the previous day's hysteria: it was as if she had exhausted all emotion. Emma wondered if she'd taken something to produce this air of composure. They stepped into the overcrowded little dwelling. Florrie's husband, Will, unusually sober, was sitting in a broken-down old armchair in a corner of the room; he nodded to the two women, but didn't speak. A baby was asleep in a wooden crib set to one side of the fire.

"I sent t' other bairns to school, they couldn't do owt here and they were only in t' way, like. Winnie's got a bit of a cold so I kept her off." She indicated the little girl who'd let Emma and Maggie in, Winnie sniffed again to prove that she did indeed have a cold.

"Emma and Maggie have made a collection for our Georgie, Will. Look, they've collected all this." She showed him the contents of the tin: "That gold sovereign is from old Hundson, what do you think of that?"

"It's to pay for t' funeral, think on, not for boozing." Emma was sorry she'd said that as soon as the words were out of her mouth, when she saw the hurt look in Will's eyes. He didn't say anything; he just nodded and turned his head away, so that the women couldn't see the weak tears in his eyes.

Georgie was in a coffin that looked heart-breakingly small, supported on two wooden kitchen chairs at the back of the room. He was dressed in a pristine white shirt that was far too big for his tiny body.

"Mrs Lawrence sent that, it was what her lad wore for his first communion, and he's grown out of it. Well he would have done, wouldn't he, he's nearly twenty now and he were only eleven when he had his first communion," Florrie explained proudly. She did a bit of cleaning for Mrs Lawrence, who lived in a large house on the north side of the town. The three women, with Winnie, looked reverently at Georgie.

"He looks like a little angel," said Emma wiping a tear from her eye with the corner of her pinny, "a little angel, bless him." After a few minutes the two neighbours took their leave, indicating they would be at the funeral on the following day.

89

It was the middle of the afternoon when the policeman came back to Audrey Thompkinson's house. Julia had persuaded her sister-in-law to wash and dress and to brush her hair, then had prepared a midday meal for them, but neither was interested in food, and it was left untouched. Ruth had kindly taken Jasper for a walk during the morning because Julia didn't feel she could leave Audrey alone in her present state; she had then returned to the big house on the cliff, promising to keep in regular contact.

Julia invited the policeman into the hall. It was Bernie

Maynard, who had broken so much bad news to relatives in the last twenty-four hours that it was becoming almost routine - but not quite. Bernie never really got hardened to it. Although Julia guessed why he had come, she wanted to break the news to Audrey in her own way.

"You've found him?" she prompted, as the young constable hesitated.

"I'm sorry, ma'am. A body was found on the beach at Cornelian Bay, and we think it is probably Mr Thompkinson. I'm very sorry," he said again.

Julia swallowed, and took a deep breath. "Do you need me to come and identify him?" she asked.

"The ... er ... body has been rather er ..." He searched for a word. "It has been damaged by the sea," he concluded lamely. Julia shuddered involuntarily.

"There are some remnants of clothing that might help, they might be enough for positive identification," volunteered the policeman.

"Thank you, this is not a pleasant task for you. I'll come to the mortuary as soon as I can leave my sister-in-law. She is not in a fit state to be left alone."

When Bernie had left, Julia went to tell Audrey the news he had brought. Audrey took the news with a calmness that completely surprised Julia.

"I knew, you know, I knew from the beginning when Jasper came home alone. I knew Geoffrey wouldn't be coming back. I didn't want to believe it, I still don't. But I can't delude myself any longer, it must be Geoffrey they've found." She began to cry, quietly at first then more wildly, Julia embraced her and the two women clung together and let their grief overwhelm them. Jasper joined them, whining piteously. After a few minutes Julia disentangled herself from Audrey's arms.

"I have to go and identify Geoffrey," she said, "will you be all right on your own for an hour or so?"

"I'm coming with you," said Audrey firmly. Julia tried to dissuade her, explaining that Geoffrey's body would be an unpleasant sight after its immersion in the sea for so long. But Audrey was determined, she seemed to have found a new strength and wasn't like the mousy little woman that Julia knew.

"I need to see him, Julia, I need to know it's really him. If I don't ... well, if I don't I'll always wonder, there'll always be a hope." Julia understood, it was how she felt herself. "All right, let's go and get it over with," she sighed as she went to get their coats.

90

"Mrs Stafford, what are you doing back here?" said Diana Fenton, as Dora was re-admitted to the ward. "I though I told you to take things easy," she scolded. Dora looked sheepish as she settled into the bed. "Well, I did try, Sister, I really did. I didn't do much really, I don't know what came over me." Dora had been found collapsed at her front door, she'd been donkey-stoning the step, when she'd felt faint and dizzy. She didn't dare tell Sister Fenton that the previous afternoon she'd cleaned and tidied the house, or that from early that morning she'd been scrubbing the kitchen floor, cooking breakfast for her family and seeing the children off to school. She had felt ill all the time, but had found it difficult to rest because there were too many demands made on her. Her husband had come home the worse for drink the previous night when she was already in bed, demanding his conjugal rights, which had been denied to him during her sojourn in hospital. There was no point in refusing him, even if she'd had the strength to do so, that would have made him violent, so she'd submitted unwillingly. It was obvious Sister Fenton was furious with her. "I'm sorry, Sister," Dora said meekly. Diana gave a loud exasperated sigh. "You stay there and do as you're told, don't you dare move until I say so!" she turned abruptly and left the bedside. "I knew this would happen, I knew it would happen," Sister Fenton blew off steam to a couple of her nurses, "she'll kill herself over that family of hers." She wasn't angry with Dora but at the circumstances that had brought her back to the ward. "It doesn't matter how long we try to keep her, she'll just have a relapse when she goes home because no-one will help her. They'll just sit back and let her kill herself." She made a sound somewhere between a snort and a sigh, as she went off to get on with her work. Meanwhile, Dora snuggled contentedly down between the starched white sheets. She hadn't really intended to come back to the hospital, but now she was here, by heck, she was going to make the most of it.

91

It took Julia and Audrey more than twenty minutes to walk to the mortuary. They had decided against taking a cab, both feeling they needed some fresh air and exercise. It was beginning to get dark when they arrived. Julia once more tried to dissuade Audrey from viewing Geoffrey's body - she had no doubt that it was Geoffrey - but Audrey was adamant. First of all they were shown some remnants of clothing, stiff and stained from immersion in the sea. Audrey gave a sob as she recognised the woollen scarf that she had knitted for Geoffrey. The mortuary attendant told them that would be adequate identification, and they did not need to see the corpse. Both women, however, knew the only way they could be absolutely positive was to see for themselves. They were shown into a dimly-lit, bare room. The outline of a body covered by a sheet could be seen lying on the table in the centre of the room. The mortuary attendant looked questioningly at the two women, Julia nodded, and he lifted one corner of the sheet. Audrey took one quick look, then with a soft moan she fell to the floor in a faint. The mortuary attendant's young assistant, who had been standing by the door, dashed across to her, but not sure what to do, he knelt, helplessly rubbing Audrey's hands with unnecessary vigour. Julia ignored her sister-in-law for a moment while she looked at Geoffrey's bloated face; she had some difficulty recognising the features of her only, beloved brother, but in spite of being in the sea for more than twenty-four hours, there was no doubt this was indeed Geoffrey. Julia nodded again and the attendant replaced the sheet, then both turned their attention to Audrey. She began to come round, moaning softly; at Julia's request the attendant sent his assistant to find a hansom cab. He sped off with alacrity, obviously relieved to leave the ministrations to someone else. The cab driver helped Julia to get Audrey into the house, and he very obligingly agreed to call in at the doctor's and ask him to visit the sickly woman. He was handsomely rewarded for his trouble with a large tip from Julia.

92

The town centre was unusually still, despite the large groups of people congregated in the streets. They stood in respectful silence as each funeral cortege passed along the road to the cemetery; the clip-clop of the horses' hooves, the sound of the carriage wheels and the occasional sobs the only noises to be heard. The cheerful decorations in the shop windows looked sadly out of place. One of the first funerals to take place was that of Gordon Harland. His parents followed the hearse, Connie tightly holding Suzie's hand, and Jim with his left arm around his wife holding Laura's hand in his right. They did not take in the surroundings until they reached the entrance to the cemetery, then Connie and Jim became aware of a group of scouts in full uniform - Gordon's scout troop - forming a guard of honour from the gates to the church doors. This moved them so much that the ready tears began to flow again. As they arrived at the church porch, the scout leader stepped forward and reverently laid the troop flag across Gordon's coffin. He placed the bush hat that Gordon had worn to meetings on top, saluted, then stood to one side to allow the family to follow the coffin into the building. The leader assembled his scouts and they marched smartly behind the cortege into church for the funeral service. Afterwards, as Gordon's coffin was lowered into the ground, a procedure that caused Connie almost to collapse in grief, his best friend from the scouts, a boy called Simon Collier, falteringly played the "Last Post" on his bugle. The flag and Gordon's hat were formally presented to Jim, who was too choked up to speak; he curtly nodded acknowledgement and turned to comfort his wife and daughters.

Later, much later, Connie would draw comfort from the fact that she had a grave to visit, when so many of her friends and neighbours would mourn for sons lost in foreign places. Those who had graves were too far away to be visited, and many had no known resting-place. But that was later, much later, not yet ... not yet, it was too soon, the grief was still too stark.

93

Later that morning, the double funeral took place of Albert Bell and Margaret Kennedy. The coffins were placed side by side on the hearse, which was followed, not only by the families of each victim, but also by a contingent of Albert's workmates, in their smart Post Office uniforms, and by the entire household of "Dunollie", including the master and mistress. Sir Robert and Lady Dorothea Brent and their three sons walked at the head of their servants. They had dismissed the coachman when he arrived at the front door with their carriage. Much to his chagrin, he had to walk with the rest of the staff. He didn't like walking.

~

It was during the afternoon that little Georgie Harrison was buried. Thanks to the generosity of friends and neighbours, his parents were able to give him a decent funeral, instead of the dreaded pauper's burial. The amount collected was not however, enough for a horse-drawn hearse. Once more, Percy's handcart was pressed into service. An old white sheet, rescued by Florrie Harrison from Mrs Lawrence's rag bag some weeks earlier, was carefully placed on the cart and the little coffin laid on top. Will Harrison and his eldest son Billy pushed the cart between them, helped up the steep hills by friends and neighbours. The sad procession passed the school where Georgie had been a pupil on the two-mile journey to the cemetery. The pupils and staff were lined up on the road outside the Friarage School; all the girls were openly crying, and all the boys were manfully trying to hold back tears, but not being very successful in most cases.

Daniel Hudson watched from his window, as Will and Billy carried the little wooden box to the waiting conveyance, followed by the rest of the family and most of the neighbours from Quay Street and all the yards around. When they'd disappeared from view, Daniel sighed and went back to his old wooden rocking chair by the fire. He did not go to the funeral with the others, and that was the last anyone saw of him.

It was on the following Sunday that Daniel's daughter Naomi, on one of her regular bi-weekly visits, found the old man. As Naomi opened the door into her father's little cottage, the chill struck her. The fire had been out a long time, the ashes grey and unwelcoming in the grate, and Daniel was sitting in his usual chair. At first, Naomi thought her father was merely sleeping, then she realised he would not wake up again. He was as cold as the surrounding atmosphere. He had been there for two days: nobody in Oxley's Yard had noticed that he hadn't been seen since little Georgie's funeral party had left the Yard on the previous Friday. Naomi was the only one who shed tears over his passing, but all his neighbours remembered his uncharacteristically generous gift to Georgie's funeral fund. Later, when Naomi sorted through her father's possessions, she found a leather pouch containing twenty-four gold sovereigns, secreted in his old ditty box, under the bed.

Like Connie Harland, earlier in the day, Florrie Harrison nearly fell into her son's grave as she saw the wooden coffin containing the body of her little boy, disappearing under clods of earth. She clung to her husband's arm as they stood close together, surrounded by their other children.

94

The final funeral for that day, was another double one. George Crowther and Leonard Firth had been friends for many years;

they often chatted in front of their respective shops at quiet times of day. Their wives had also become friends and the two couples met socially at least once a week. Kathy Crowther and Nancy Firth walked with heads bowed, arm-in-arm behind the hearse, with their respective families following. Kathy had a son and a daughter both still at school. Nancy had two tall sons, one of whom, Lawrence, was in the army and was on compassionate leave to attend his father's funeral. Perhaps it was fortunate that Nancy was unable to see into the future. Her beloved elder son was destined to perish at the battle of the Somme at the age of twenty-two. The two widows shared their grief and comforted each other, as their husbands were laid side by side in adjoining graves.

95

For the third day gangs of workmen were clearing away debris. Bob West's group had, like many others, spent all the previous day sifting through rubbish, demolishing unsafe walls and generally trying to bring some sort of order from the chaos of the bombardment. They had found no more bodies or injured people since late on Wednesday afternoon, much to their relief. They were now assessing the damage to the Bensons' house: part of the wall at the side of the house had gone, and there was a hole from the roof to the cellar where a shell had gone all the way through. There would be a lot of work to make the house habitable again, but in Bob's estimation it wouldn't have to be completely demolished and rebuilt.

"What's that noise"? asked Frank Porter suddenly: everyone stopped and listened, but they couldn't hear anything, so they resumed work. "There it is again," said Frank, "it sounded like a bairn crying."

"Nay," said Cec Lindhurst, "can't be, they were all accounted for. They didn't have no more bairns." As he was speaking there came a distinct cry. "It's coming from over here." Bob went to the fireplace and listened as the cry came again: "It's coming from in here," he said as he opened the door of the fire oven. Timmy, the Bensons' cat jumped out, mewing his thanks to his rescuers. "Bloody Hell, it must have been there since Wednesday morning, poor little bugger," said Cec. "Here pussy," he opened one of the sandwiches he'd brought for his dinner, took out a slice of meat and offered it to Timmy. The cat ate it ravenously. Several other men took out their sandwiches, and followed suit. Someone found a chipped saucer and filled it with water for the thirsty cat.

"I'll take him round to Cissie Wellings, she's got Chris Benson staying there with her."

"Why, that's a miracle," said Cissie when Bob put Timmy into her arms, explaining how he'd been found, "fancy him thinking to hide in the oven," she said wonderingly. She had briefly wondered what had happened to the cat, and assumed he'd been buried under a pile of bricks with the family. Chris was still sitting by the fire, apathetically staring at nothing. Gently Cissie placed Timmy into his arms.

"Look Chris, Bob West found Timmy hiding in the oven, he's been there more than two days." There was no reaction, Cissie sighed. "I'll get him something to eat, he'll be starving, poor little mite. I've got a bit of liver he can have." She went off to the kitchen end of the living room, where she busied herself chopping up the liver and pouring milk into a saucer. She turned, and stopped in the act of putting the plate of meat and saucer of milk down on the floor. Timmy was lying on Chris's chest nuzzling his neck, and purring loudly. Cissie stared as Chris gently began to stroke the cat; a tear slowly coursed down his cheek, then another, which fell on

Timmy's fur. The cat indignantly jumped off Christopher's knee, and ran to where Cissie had hurriedly put down the plate and saucer as she went over to Chris. She knelt on the hearthrug and took hold of his hands. The tears were flowing freely now Chris wept unrestrainedly, his body shaking convulsively with his sobs.

"That's right, lad, that's right, let it all come out," Cissie wept with her nephew, as she knelt by his chair and took him in her arms. Timmy, replete from his second feed in less than twenty minutes, strolled back to the fire. Ignoring the two distressed humans, he washed himself, then lay down on the home-made clippy rug, and purring contentedly fell asleep, his recent ordeal apparently completely forgotten.

It wasn't so easy for Cissie and Christopher, the tears flowed as if they would never stop. They released all of the pent-up emotion of the last two days.

"She came for him, you know," Chris sobbed, his words almost unintelligible.

"What?" asked Cissie, these were the first words her nephew had spoken since the tragedy. "What did you say, love?"

"Me Mam, she was there in t' hospital." He tried to control his emotion as he told her.

"Just before he died, me Dad ... he said, 'I'm coming love', then ... then he went ... I never saw her myself - but she was there. She was," he added fiercely as if he wouldn't be believed. Christopher's whole body shook as he went into another paroxysm of weeping.

"Aye lad, aye. I believe you," Cissie said earnestly as she tried to comfort him. They were still clinging together weeping quietly when Duggie, Cissie's husband, returned home from his few days' fishing at sea. Until then he had been blissfully unaware of the tragedy that awaited him at home. He'd seen all the damage inflicted on the sea front and had seen the lighthouse without its majestic glass dome, and had heard talk of people being killed, but hadn't expected his wife's family to be so tragically involved. This was the sort of thing that happened to other people.

96

Mrs Gregory had spent most of the last two days clearing the debris from Fiona Cameron's room, and the glazier had just finished replacing the window.. Although it was against Amelia's principles to go looking through other people's private possessions, this was an exception. It was necessary to find who was Fiona's next of kin. On Thursday morning, feeling that she was intruding, she steeled herself to inspect the contents of a small polished wooden box she found in the sideboard cupboard in Fiona's room. Inside the box was a pocket-sized, well-used Bible, a diary and some letters. Mrs Gregory did not open the diary, neither did she read the letters, she only took note of the Edinburgh address at the top of the page and saw they were signed "your loving father and mother." Not quite knowing what to do next, Mrs Gregory thought the best thing to do was to go round to the police station with the information and ask them if they could let Fiona's parents know what had happened. The Sergeant at the desk was most obliging and informed the concerned landlady that he would telegraph the Edinburgh police immediately.

Mrs Gregory was preparing her midday meal on Saturday when she was interrupted by an authoritative knock at the front door. The caller was a distinguished-looking gentleman who looked to be in his late fifties. Even before he spoke, Mrs Gregory knew who he was. He raised his hat. "Mrs

Gregory?" he asked with a pronounced Scottish accent. "I am James Cameron," he went on as she nodded. "Oh yes, yes, Fiona's father, please come in, come in do." Mrs Gregory was rather flustered, she hadn't expected a visit, even though she had written a note of condolence to Fiona's parents. James Cameron politely refused any refreshment, stating he had to catch the next train back to Edinburgh and was unable to stay more than a few minutes.

"I came down to take Fiona and her baby back home," he explained. "I arrived late last night and stayed in a hotel near the railway station. I wanted to thank you for everything you did for them." He paused: "Very few people would take in an unmarried mother, you are a very Christian lady." He went on to tell her that until the police had informed them about the two deaths, he and his wife had not known about the baby.

"Fiona told us she had obtained employment in a children's home in Yorkshire. We didn't know. We never suspected."

"Would you have taken her in or turned her away if you had known?" asked Mrs Gregory boldly. This took Mr Cameron by surprise, but he was not offended by the question. "I don't know, Mrs Gregory, I honestly don't know. I hope that I would have acted like a Christian, but I don't know." The man was obviously deeply distressed, Mrs Gregory felt very sorry for him. "There are one or two personal mementoes belonging to Fiona that I'm sure you'd like to take with you. I have packed up all her clothes and Heather's too, you must let me know what you want doing with them."

"Heather, is that the baby's name? We didn't know. Heather, Heather," he murmured.

"She said it reminded her of Scotland," answered Mrs Gregory gently. She excused herself while she went to fetch the small box in which Fiona's Bible and diary were enclosed, there was also a velvet-covered bag containing some inexpensive trinkets. James Cameron said he would arrange to have the remainder of his daughter's possessions collected and despatched to Edinburgh as soon as it could be arranged, then thanking the kindly landlady he shook her hand and took his leave, to begin the sad journey home to his grieving wife.

"What a waste, what a waste," Amelia Gregory said to herself when she returned to her kitchen to finish preparing her lunch, though she didn't really feel like eating. "If she'd had the courage to tell her parents, and if they'd looked after her, Fiona and Heather would both be alive today. So many 'ifs'. What a waste of young lives," she wept quietly as she filled the kettle and put it on the hob.

97

"She looks so beautiful." John found it almost impossible to believe that his fiancée was really dead, she looked as if she was merely sleeping. Anne, lying in her coffin, was wearing the dress that she should have been married in that very day; instead this was her funeral. Four guests, who had travelled from Leeds, arrived prepared for a wedding, unaware of the bride's death. They had heard about the bombardment but it had never entered their heads that their own family would be involved. Instead of the anticipated joyous occasion they found they were to attend Anne's funeral; their colourful wedding clothes looked conspicuous amongst the black-clad mourners. Mr and Mrs Ellis and John too, assured the embarrassed guests that it didn't matter what they were wearing, they couldn't have known, and there had been no time to inform them, indeed no-one had thought to do so in the midst of their grief.

"Anne wouldn't object at all," said her mother, "she loved bright colours," but even so, they couldn't help feeling out of place, until friends and neighbours looked through wardrobes and found enough suitably sombre garments for them to borrow.

Just before the coffin was closed, without anyone noticing, John took the wedding ring he had bought for his bride-to-be from the top pocket of his jacket, and quietly slipped it on to the third finger of Anne's left hand.

"I'll always think of you as my wife," he whispered softly, so no one else could hear. "I'll always love you."

98

Iris woke up at her usual time on Saturday morning, and stretched out in the bed, knowing that she did not have to get up too early. Today was her fourteenth birthday, she felt a mixture of excitement and sadness. Excited because she was now grown-up, and in a few days' time would leave school, then there was Christmas to look forward to, although it wouldn't be much of a celebration this year. On the Monday after Christmas she would start work as an apprentice milliner. She felt very melancholy, however, when she thought about all the casualties of the bombardment, and all the damage that had been done. Really the Appleby family had been very lucky; two front windows of the house had been broken, other than that there had been no damage to their property, and the family had survived without injury. She had watched Percy's cart leave from Sandside the previous day, taking little Georgie Harrison to the cemetery, and had sobbed as if her heart would break. She had also stood on the pavement and watched as other funeral processions wended their way to the burial ground. Even though she did not know all the victims or their families, she wept with other onlookers. The church social that Iris had so been looking forward to for several weeks had been cancelled as a mark of respect; she was disappointed but knew that it was the right thing to do while the air of dejection and mourning prevailed. Iris sighed, got out of bed, and began to dress; she was eager to see what birthday presents she might have. A letter had arrived the previous morning; her mother had quickly hidden it but not before Iris had seen the colourful foreign stamp. She knew it was from her father who would no doubt bring her an exotic present when he returned from his trip to Buenos Aires.

99

Saturday morning saw the funeral of Herbert Wedderburn. Emily, grim-faced and holding a daughter by each hand, nodded curtly to her late husband's family and friends, but kept her distance. There were few mourners, Herbert did not have many friends and came from a small family. There was nobody from Emily's side of the family. The service was short; at the committal, Emily stood apart from Herbert's relatives, and as soon as the coffin was lowered into the ground, she abruptly left the graveside with a bewildered Phoebe and Sophia. Beattie, sobbing in her husband's arms, did not even notice her sister-in-law's departure. The others were disconcerted by Emily's behaviour, they had at least expected to be invited back to Herbert's house. Arthur quickly took charge of the situation and asked everyone to go home with him and Beattie. Nothing was actually prepared but he knew there was plenty of food in the house as Beattie had spent the last few weeks stocking up for Christmas.

Norman Soames did not attend Herbert's funeral; he had to keep the chemist shop open, on Emily's orders. He was quite relieved really; he would rather be working than making last farewells to his late employer, whom he barely tolerated. Norman wondered what the future held for him, he did not particularly care for Mrs Wedderburn's attitude and was not looking forward to the prospect of working for her. He was considering joining the army, he thought maybe his pharmaceutical qualifications would be useful in the medical corps.

If Emily Wedderburn had given any thought to what had happened to her husband's mistress, which of course she didn't, she would have learned that Irene's body had been taken by her sister for burial in the family plot, in a little village churchyard on the Yorkshire Wolds.

100

It was Sunday morning before Stella Reynolds regained consciousness completely; she gradually became fully aware of her surroundings, and a nurse hearing her strangled cry hurried over.

"Ah, awake at last. And how are you feeling?" she asked briskly, as she took Stella's wrist and felt her pulse. Stella was bewildered, she knew she was in hospital but had no idea how she came to be there. "What's happened, what am I doing here?" she asked the nurse, a large bustling lady who had the inappropriate name of Grace Lightly. Grace avoided answering the question. "Don't worry," she ordered, her hearty voice booming round the ward, startling to wakefulness some patients who were dozing. "I'm sure you'd like a nice cup of tea, wouldn't you?" Without waiting for an answer, she bustled off, to return in a few moments with a steaming cup, which she placed on the bedside table while she carefully helped Stella to a sitting position. Stella winced with pain as she was moved, "Oh, my leg," she cried involuntarily. "Yes, you'll soon be better, you'll soon be all right," Grace soothed. "But what happened?" Stella was becoming frustrated at not having her questions answered. She tried to remember, but the effort made her head ache. "Doctor will be coming to see you soon and you'll be having visitors this afternoon as usual. Your mum and dad have been every day since you were brought in, and there've been other visitors too." Grace skilfully avoided answering Stella's questions. Stella gave up trying to get information, the effort was making her head ache again. She decided to wait for the doctor, to see if he was more forthcoming. Stella sipped her tea, but her hand was shaking so much she spilled some of the hot liquid down the front of her nightdress, so she gave up the struggle, and replaced the cup on the bedside locker. The doctor was no more informative than the nurse had been, he gave her a cursory examination, and told her she was doing well, then left. Stella waited impatiently for visiting hour; her mother was first in, closely followed by Anne's fiancé John. She gave a cry of relief when she saw her daughter was fully conscious, and sitting up in bed after four days of being partially comatose. Mrs Reynolds burst into tears as she took Stella's hand. "Oh mum, don't. Tell me what's happened, no one will tell me anything. Oh hallo, John," she said with some surprise as she saw him standing just behind her mother. "Do you remember anything, love?" asked her mother, "do you remember going to work on Wednesday?"

"Wednesday? What's today then?" Stella was confused. "Anne and I were crossing the road to go into the shop and then ... then, I don't know, I can't remember. Why can't I remember?" her voice rose hysterically. Choosing their words carefully, Mrs Reynolds and John told Stella all that had happened. She accepted the loss of her leg with better equanimity than she accepted the news that Anne had been killed. "Oh John, poor John, she was so excited, she was so looking forward to you coming. Oh Anne, Anne." She sobbed so much that her mother and John became alarmed. Grace Lightly came quickly to help comfort her; she held Stella against her ample bosom and stroked her hair, murmuring soothing platitudes as she did so. Eventually Stella calmed down, and as Grace left the bedside, asked for more details of the previous Wednesday's events. Grace allowed the visitors to stay a few minutes after visiting hour was officially over, by which time Stella was quite composed. "Come again soon," she pleaded, as her mother and John stood up and turned to leave. "We shall be here this evening, your father and I, and I shall come every afternoon as well," Mrs Reynolds assured her. "Your father will have to go back to work tomorrow so he won't be able to come during the day. He'll be so pleased that you are awake again. He's waiting downstairs for us, you aren't allowed more than two visitors at a time, and John wanted to see you."

"And I shall come again soon, if I may," said John as he kissed her lightly on the cheek. "Yes do John, please come again." Stella clung to his hand for a few minutes before letting him go.

Mr Reynolds was anxiously waiting for them near the hospital entrance. He had generously let John visit in his stead, as he would see his daughter in the evening. He had been every visiting hour since Stella had been admitted, sitting quietly with his wife and willing Stella to wake up and speak to them. Mr Reynolds was cheered when he heard that Stella had at last fully regained consciousness, but upset when he heard how distressed she was. "Well, it's only to be expected isn't it? There's no easy way of breaking news like that." He put his arm round his weeping wife. "Come on, lass, she's getting better, it was more than we hoped for a couple of days ago." He turned to John. "I'm sorry it didn't turn out as well for you lad, I'm so sorry." His voice broke. John, unable to answer, touched him on the shoulder and the three of them left the hospital until the next visiting hour later that day.

101

The hospital staff on the children's ward were pleased with the progress made by young Raymond. With a resilience that seems to be inbred in children, once he had come round properly after the operation to amputate his foot, he went from strength to strength. His parents and other members of the family had taken it in turns to visit every day; they were so relieved that their little boy was not going to die that the loss of a foot seemed relatively unimportant. Raymond had accepted his disability immediately, he seemed to be enjoying the attention. Those children on the ward who were allowed out of bed kept coming to look at his bandaged stump, the others craned their necks to see from their beds. Raymond was only too happy to show it off at every opportunity, he was too young to worry about his future life with only one foot. He had not yet been told about Georgie's death, and surprisingly he had made no reference to his friend. It had been tacitly agreed between the family and hospital staff that no mention would be made of the events leading up to Raymond being in hospital, until he himself brought up the subject.

102

Every church in the town was more crowded than usual that Sunday morning. At the twelfth century parish church near the castle, every pew was full. Dulcie and Charlotte Morgan were there with both parents. Mr Morgan did not go to church very often, he usually made the excuse that he was too busy. Dulcie wished she could get away with the same excuse, but no matter what ingenious reasons she came up with Mrs Morgan would not accept any one of them. She couldn't wait to be grown-up, then she could do exactly as she liked. Dulcie had grumbled that they had to walk much further than usual and leave much earlier than usual to come to St. Mary's instead of going to St. Martin's, their regular place of worship. "We could have at least gone in a carriage. It's bitterly cold, we'll freeze to death going all that way *and* we have to leave *hours* earlier," Dulcie had informed her sister when told of the change of arrangements, but her mother had insisted the family walk the length of the Esplanade, across the Spa Bridge, along St. Nicholas Cliff, passing the damaged Grand and Royal hotels and eventually up Castle Road to the Church. "A good brisk walk will do you the world of good," she informed her husband and daughters, "and do not exaggerate, Dulcie," she added, overhearing her daughter's last remark. Mr Morgan just grunted, but did not argue, he had found out long ago that arguing with his wife was a futile exercise.

"Do you know, when I'm grown up I shall *never* go to church again," Dulcie declared, as she walked hand in hand with her sister a few steps behind their parents.

"What about when you get married, and when you have your babies christened? You'll have to go to church then," Charlotte argued, "and when grandma and grandpa die you'll have to go to the funerals."

"I am never going to get married or have babies," was

Dulcie's emphatic reply, "but I will go to the funerals," she conceded. When she was twenty-two, Dulcie married a young curate, had four children and eventually became a Bishop's wife as her husband progressed up the church hierarchy.

During the walk they were able to see for the first time the extent of the devastation caused by the bombardment, as they came to the town centre. This had the welcome effect of temporarily silencing Dulcie, so shocked was she by the sight of badly damaged buildings on their route.

The service was much longer than the normal Sunday morning worship. Dulcie and Charlotte were admonished several times for fidgeting. They did, however, listen intently when the vicar paid homage to the victims of the bombardment: he read out the names of the eighteen people who had been killed, including that of their neighbour Mrs Temple. Dulcie and Charlotte cried quietly when they heard that some children, including a baby, had died. Several members of the congregation had tears in their eyes, and many more were openly crying. Until that moment the events of the previous Wednesday had seemed a rather exciting diversion with just a hint of danger, to Dulcie and Charlotte. They had been shocked by Mrs Temple's death but she was grown up, and being in her fifties quite old really, so they were able to accept that. To hear that children younger than themselves had been killed, filled them with horror and dismay. The girls had not been allowed to read the newspapers and their parents had not spoken of the disaster in their presence. The girls at school had not known many of the details either, so this was the first they had heard of how devastating the attack on the town had really been. It was a very subdued Morgan family who walked back home for their Sunday dinner. Later in the afternoon, Mrs Morgan retired to the sitting room to write letters; her husband occupied himself in his study in ways known only to himself. Dulcie and Charlotte were supposed to be sitting quietly in their bedroom reading books suitable for the Sabbath, but Dulcie sneaked down to the kitchen by the back stairs when she knew cook would be having her regular Sunday afternoon nap. She persuaded Mary the maid to search through the newspapers kept for lighting fires, to see if those for the previous three days were still there. They were all still intact; cook had put them to one side and kept them as souvenirs. Promising to return them shortly, Dulcie crept back to the bedroom where Charlotte was anxiously waiting, and the two girls spent the afternoon absorbing the full details of all that had happened. They included a report of the steeple of their own church being struck while they themselves were actually inside the building. "Gosh, we could have been killed too if we'd been just outside," said Dulcie. Charlotte just nodded.

103

Stan Merriman opened his shop as usual on the Monday morning following the bombardment. Unsmilingly he served his customers, nodding curtly whenever condolences were expressed and speaking only when absolutely necessary. He had refused all offers of help, which meant that the women had to wait much longer than usual to be served. They all understood, and waited patiently and uncomplainingly, talking to each other in low voices; even the voluble Mrs Braithwaite's usual bombastic attitude had been replaced by a much more subdued air. Dolly's funeral on Saturday afternoon had been attended by all the Merrimans' regular patrons, as well as relatives and friends, including Seth Adams and Henry Pike. Stan hardly noticed who was there, his eyes never left Dolly's coffin, and he was entirely unaware of what was going on around him, until he heard the vicar mention an unfamiliar name. "Dorothy May? What on earth is he talking about?" Stan thought angrily. "Who the hell is Dorothy May?" Then he remembered his wedding day, the last time his Dolly had been called by her given name, and he had been called Stanley Thomas. He'd smiled when he heard it then, she'd smiled back. Today it made him angry, she was Dolly, his Dolly, and that was how she should have been referred to on this occasion. Stan stood at the graveside until the coffin was completely concealed by soil, then, without a word to anyone he abruptly left the cemetery and returned to the flat above the shop, leaving the other mourners no alternative than to disperse uncertainly and return to their respective homes.

Henry Pike had visited Stan each day since Dolly's death. Henry felt that he was helping Stan just by being there. Most of the time the two men sat in silence, occasionally they talked. Henry did most of the talking at first, he told Stan about his work on the pier, and about his family. At first Stan gave no indication that he was listening, then he began to nod at intervals in acknowledgement of something Henry had said, occasionally making a comment or asking a question. Stan appreciated the company of someone who was not a member of the family and gradually began to contribute more to their conversations. For some reason he found it easier to talk to a comparative stranger. Within a very short time the two men ceased to be strangers and became firm friends in spite of the difference in their ages. A friendship that was to last for the rest of Stan's life.

104

Geoffrey Thompkinson's funeral was a very quiet affair. Two work colleagues, Mr Wentworth and Mr Lomas, came to represent the firm where Geoffrey had spent all his working life. They brought with them a large wreath on behalf of all the management and employees. There were a couple of distant cousins of Audrey's and three middle-aged couples with whom Geoffrey and Audrey had infrequently played Whist or Bridge. Julia was touched and grateful when Richard Lovell and Ruth Jenkins arrived in Richard's motor car, bearing a wreath which had a card attached expressing their condolences. Audrey had to be supported by Julia and Mr Wentworth, Geoffrey's second-in-command, who would now be rather reluctantly promoted; he had told his wife he did not like the idea of "stepping into a dead man's shoes." Nevertheless he did not refuse the rise in status. After the service and committal, Julia, on Audrey's behalf invited the mourners back to the house for refreshments. Mr Wentworth and his colleague, Mr Lomas, politely declined and excused themselves, they had regretfully to return to their work. They expressed their condolences once more on behalf of themselves and the firm, and said they would keep in touch. Audrey never heard from them again.

105

It was not until Wednesday, a full week after the bombardment, that the final funerals took place. It had taken time to arrange for four burials at the same time. Large crowds, mainly women, lined the streets all the way from Cissie Welling's house to the church, and from the church to the cemetery. No one could ever remember four members of one family being buried at the same time. The Bensons were quite well known in the community and the majority came genuinely to mourn them, a few were merely curious, wondering what the face of a young man who had lost all his immediate family would look like. If they were expecting to see someone bowed down or demented with grief, they were disappointed. Christopher, dressed in his full naval uniform, carried himself with a quiet dignity. His physical injuries were beginning to heal - the mental and emotional ones would take much longer - and he limped along on his still-painful ankle without the aid of a stick. He had refused to ride in a carriage with Cissie and two more female relatives, but his Uncle Duggie walked alongside him, and both men stared straight ahead, no emotion registering on their faces. Not one of the onlookers could imagine the turmoil behind those bleak expressions. There were two hearses, each carrying one small and one larger coffin. There was the sound of subdued sobbing from women who were complete strangers, moved by the sight of the cortege; many of their menfolk had trouble holding back the tears. Kathleen Davison was among the mourners walking behind the hearse with the family. She had considered taking Patrick with her, but he would have been confused and bewildered. She had left him placidly working at his never-ending knitting, slipping out quietly while he was occupied. Their daughter Joanna was keeping an eye on him, Patrick wouldn't be happy when he realised it was Joanna and not Kathleen who was looking after him, but she had to come.

As the mourners began to drift away from the graveside after the multiple committal, Christopher suddenly brought himself to attention and gave a smart salute. "I'll get the bastards for you, I'll get 'em," he muttered. No one could hear him, those who saw his lips move assumed he was saying a short prayer. He turned away, and flanked by Cissie and Duggie, left the cemetery.

106

For most of the adult population, and indeed for some of the children, Christmas 1914 was not the happy time it usually was. Too much loss had been sustained too recently, for the pain to start receding. Even those who had not been directly affected by the bombardment celebrated the season in a subdued frame of mind. Many mothers were apprehensive and distressed by the sudden patriotic fervour of their sons, who had been influenced by the posters which were appearing on hoardings and walls, not just in Scarborough but all over the country. Posters which exhorted those who loved their country to "Remember Scarborough! Enlist now!" Still in a state of shock and anger at the outrage wrought on their town, the number of young men who had volunteered for active service was quite phenomenal.

107

Connie and Jim Harland tried to make Christmas Day as happy as possible for the sake of their two little girls. The presents already bought and wrapped for Gordon were upstairs in his bedroom; as yet, they had given no thought about what to do with them. Suzie and Laura exclaimed delightedly as they opened each of their presents, but their joy was forced. "I do wish Gordon was here," said Suzie wistfully. Connie, thinking of the small pile of presents that Gordon would never receive, could no longer hold her emotions in check and began to sob. Jim put his arms around his wife, Laura and Suzie came closer and he drew them into his embrace. The family clung together in grief and wept.

108

To the Harrison family, Christmas was hardly distinguishable from any other day of the year. Florrie and Will couldn't afford to buy presents for their children at any time of year: birthdays went by unremarked and uncelebrated, and Christmas was no different. The other families in the yards were in the same circumstances; they concentrated on trying to keep warm and adequately fed, but were not always successful. The festive season hardly intruded into their lives. The Turners were the only family in Oxley's Yard to do anything out of the ordinary on that Yuletide: they visited Raymond in hospital during the afternoon.

109

The hospital had been gaily decorated to cheer up the patients who had to stay there over the Christmas period. A large tree stood in the corner of the children's ward and there was an air of subdued excitement among the young patients. Matron Richardson had relaxed the rules a little and was allowing not just parents, but children also to visit for two hours in the afternoon. This indulgence was extended to some of the other wards. The visiting rules in the maternity ward had not, however, been relaxed; new-born babies could not risk being exposed to infection by visitors, though what happened after they went home was no concern of the hospital staff. A baby boy had been born in the early hours of the morning, much to the delight, not only of his parents but of the ward staff as well. The very seriously-ill patients were segregated from the rest and the strict visiting rules still applied to them.

Matron toured the wards from mid-morning, graciously wishing each individual patient a Happy Christmas. Ward Sister Diana Fenton had made sure Dora Stafford was not discharged before Christmas, knowing her husband and family would again take advantage of her. The doctor thought that Dora would be well enough to go home, but Diana had argued with him that her home conditions were not conducive to convalescing and it would be wiser to keep her in hospital. In the end the doctor acquiesced: he was rather in awe of Sister Fenton. Dora's family visited her during the afternoon. She sat up in bed trying to look more ill than she actually was, so that her family would realise her prolonged sojourn in hospital was justified. Diana Fenton kept an eagle eye on all the visitors, not wanting her ward disrupted or any of her patients upset. When all her family had gone, Dora confided to Diana that it was the best Christmas she could remember.

"No cooking, no clearing up, and 'im not coming in drunk. It were lovely. I think I'll try and be in here every Christmas," she gave a deep sight of contentment, "this is what heaven must be like."

"Well, she's the first patient I've ever met that would rather be in hospital than at home at Christmas - or at any other time for that matter," Diana commented to her ward staff.

110

Ruth Jenkins invited Julia and Audrey Thompkinson, and Jasper, to tea at the big house on the cliff. Audrey, still very much wallowing in her grief, did not want to go, but Julia although at first reluctant to accept herself, finally succeeded in persuading her sister-in-law. She thought a change of scenery and the company of other people would be a diversion from their sorrowing. Julia's surmise proved correct, and it turned out to be an unexpectedly pleasant afternoon for both of them. They got to know Richard better, having previously met him only briefly at Geoffrey's funeral. Both women thought he was very charming. They met his children, excited by the occasion and wanting to show the two guests their Christmas gifts, and found them enchanting. No communication had been received from their mother, but as her memory had faded from their mind, this did not disturb them. They played with Jasper, who was delighted to be the centre of their attention: he wagged his tail and allowed himself to be stroked and patted. Richard's sister Louise called in with her husband and family, in the middle of the afternoon, to wish her brother and his children the season's greetings, and to bring more presents for their niece and nephew. They remained only a short time and did not stay for tea.

Julia and Audrey were fascinated by Richard's telescope and gasped in amazement at being able to see so much detail on the ships in the harbour, and to be able to see landmarks along the coast so clearly. Richard was careful not to train the lens onto the cliffs where Geoffrey had met his death; nothing was mentioned about the occurrence. In the early evening, the two ladies took their leave, declining their host's offer to have them driven home.

"It isn't far and the walk will do us good. Thank you for your offer and thank you very much for a lovely afternoon, we have enjoyed it so much," said Julia as she and Audrey shook hands with Richard and Ruth as they departed.

"Yes, thank you so much," echoed Audrey.

"I didn't think I would enjoy anything so soon after ..." she couldn't bring herself to say the words, "but I did." Julia squeezed her sister-in-law's hand, understanding exactly what Audrey meant. It was quite a pleasant evening for a walk, the air was clear and frosty, hundreds of stars twinkled like diamonds in the sky. Jasper, free from the restraint of his lead, kept running a few yards in front of the two women then running back to them. Julia wondered if this evening would be a good time to broach the subject of Audrey's future, but as she did not have to be back in Manchester for another ten days she could afford to wait a little while longer. Both women were now virtually alone; Julia was going to suggest that Audrey came to live with her in Manchester. She did not really want to do this, she much preferred living alone and living her life as she wanted to. She didn't want the burden of her sister-in-law, but felt it was her duty to offer Audrey a home.

111

Brian and Donald Hollis had the best Christmas they could remember. Miss Fox had invited them with their mother to spend the whole day with her. It was also the best Christmas Miss Fox had had for many years. The day was usually spent in the same way as every other day of the year. Mr and Mrs Barton were flabbergasted to see their employer so animated; they'd never seen her like this in all the years they had worked for her. Sarah felt rather out of her depth, she sat awkwardly on the edge of her chair not quite sure how to behave. The boys had no inhibitions and soon their mother began to relax slightly as she observed their excitement. Miss Fox had given the two boys a wooden fort, which many years before had belonged to her brothers. During the previous day, Mr Barton had been requested to retrieve the fort from the attic where it had been stored for so long. Mrs Barton had dusted it, and it looked as good as ever. There were also some more soldiers to add to their collection, and Brian and Donald were delighted with their gifts. Mr and Mrs Barton had been invited to join Miss Fox, Sarah and the boys for lunch. They declined giving the reason that Mrs Barton preferred to stay in the kitchen to keep an eye on the progress of the cooking. There was so much to eat at dinner, Brian and Donald felt they would never be hungry again, but by late afternoon they were ready for their tea. They were given some fruit, cakes and sweets to take home with them. The empty house was very cold, not having had a fire in it all day, so they all went straight to bed, and within minutes of climbing they were fast asleep, satiated and contented.

Miss Fox sat alone by her bedroom fire, contemplating the events of the day; she couldn't remember when was the last time she had enjoyed herself like that. She thought of Christmases past when she and her brothers had been children. "Charles, Oliver," she murmured and the tears slowly ran, unchecked, down her cheeks.

112

Walter Slack spent another convivial day with Hilda and Cyril, and their sons, Adam and Timothy. In honour of the occasion he wore his one good suit, complete with clean white shirt and starched collar. Nutty had had the suit for almost a quarter of a century; he had first worn it to his wedding, then five years later to his young wife's funeral, since then it had been out of his wardrobe on only three other occasions, one christening and two more funerals. The journey to his brother's smallholding was taken at a more leisurely pace than on the previous occasion when poor old Plodder had bolted in fright. Almost as soon as Nutty entered Cyril's house he removed the unaccustomed stiff collar, which was beginning to chafe the back of his neck. The table was heavily laden with a succulent roast goose, and fresh vegetables grown in their own smallholding, followed by a large home-made plum pudding covered in brandy sauce. Plodder was not forgotten, he was housed in the large outhouse and given plenty of bran mash and water, and was quite contented. Walter, Cyril and his two sons did justice to Hilda's cooking, and so gorged were they after a massive mid-day meal that the whole family slept the afternoon away. They woke up about five o'clock ready to tackle the home-cured ham, and home-made bread topped with creamy yellow butter, followed by the mountain of cakes and scones Hilda had baked, and washed down with several cups of strong well-sugared tea. Cyril's home brewed beer gave no signs of running out and Hilda's cooking as always was perfect. Nutty had never felt so satisfied and once more brought up the subject of retirement. The two brothers talked at length about the prospect but made no firm plans, which was no surprise to Hilda. Once more it was left to Plodder to see Nutty safely home, so full of food and drink was he that he could hardly move on his own. It was with great difficulty that he unharnessed Plodder and led him into the stable. Nutty spent the night fully clothed on top of his bed, to wake shivering and bleary-eyed at six o'clock the following morning. By eight o'clock, Nutty was back at work on his rounds as usual.

113

Mrs Mason had claimed the most comfortable chair, nearest the fire, in her son's home, and left it only when necessary throughout the whole of the Christmas period. Enid established herself cosily on the opposite side of the hearth to her mother. Marianne was not at all pleased, and complained loudly and incessantly to her long-suffering husband, who wanted only to keep the peace. True to her word, Enid had not lifted a finger to help her sister-in-law, using her broken arm and bruises as her excuse, not to mention the recurring blinding headaches she had suffered from since the bombardment. Marianne was not sure how much of this was true. "She's as bad as your mother with her imaginary aches and pains," she wailed to Roger. She had informed her friends that they would not be able to visit over Christmas, giving the reason that Mrs Mason and Enid were suffering the after-effects of being buried under their house during the bombardment, and hinting that she did not want them to be unduly upset. Her friends said they understood, and thought Marianne was being very noble and self-sacrificing. In reality she was afraid of being shown up by her mother-in-law and sister-in-law. While Mrs Mason and Enid had an enjoyable time - Enid especially liked being waited on instead of having to do all the running around - Marianne tight-lipped and furious hated every minute. "How much longer are they going to stay?" she demanded of her husband through gritted teeth. Roger, trying to keep the peace between his wife and his mother and sister, was almost a nervous wreck and he certainly did not enjoy Christmas at all that year.

114

Jack and Gwen Watson spent a very quiet Christmas together. There were brief visits from the family during the morning, but, having previously been told by their mother how ill their father was, they stayed only long enough for the adults to have a small glass of sherry and for the children to have some homemade ginger wine. Jack and Gwen, both knowing that this was their last Christmas together, wanted to spend as much precious time as possible, alone. They spent the afternoon talking in a leisurely way about the past, of their youth, their marriage, and their children. There was no future for them to speak of, as a couple.

"But you'll manage, love, you'll mange, won't you lass?" Jack patted his wife's knee.

"Of course I will, don't you worry, I'll be alright. I've managed without you afore," she said, but thought to herself, that in the past, he always came back after an absence. "Now what about a nice cup of tea and some cake?" Gwen said briskly as she got up to fill the kettle, turning her face away from him so that he wouldn't see the tears in her eyes. It turned out to be their last day together; Jack died peacefully in his sleep the same night.

115

"I think it's too soon for you to go back. You're not well enough, I'm sure they'd let you stay longer if you asked," Cissie Wellings said to her nephew. "Mebbe they would, Auntie Cissie, mebbe they would, but I want to go back. I need to go, I can't explain why." Christopher had told his aunt and uncle only the previous evening of his decision to return to his shore base.

His sick leave was indefinite until his injuries were properly healed. He still walked with a slight limp, but most of his cuts had healed and the bruises had faded. The emotional damage would take much longer to remedy. Chris felt he needed to be doing something, he had the idea that returning to active service would give him the opportunity to avenge the deaths of his parents and his little brothers. He wasn't sure how he could actually achieve this, but the inaction was making him more and more depressed each day. Although she tried to persuade him to stay, Cissie had an inkling of how he was feeling. She realised he needed to be doing something to stop him from brooding; she felt the same way herself. "I'll come to t' station with you, love." She reached for her coat. "No!" She stopped in mid-action. Chris had not intended to sound so abrupt. "No, Auntie Cissie," he repeated more gently, "please, I'd rather go on my own." He did not want any emotional farewells in a public place. "All right, love, I understand." Cissie hugged him close and kissed him as she wept. Chris disentangled himself and after a brief handshake with Duggie, he left without another word.

116

John Somerford had allowed only his brother Michael to accompany him to the station; like Christopher Benson he too wanted to avoid any moving leave-takings, and had dissuaded his parents from seeing him off. Michael could be trusted to keep his feelings in check. The train was not too crowded. John chose a compartment occupied by a sailor sitting quietly in a corner seat, staring out of the window; he did not look up when John threw his kitbag on to the rack, put his overcoat on the seat opposite then went back on to the platform to say "goodbye" to his brother. The brothers embraced briefly, then Michael left, turning at the ticket barrier to give a final wave, before he handed over his platform ticket to the morose Billy Bowman.

Christopher looked up as John re-entered the compartment; he noticed the black armband on the army sergeant's sleeve. Chris was also wearing a mourning band, but it did not show up so clearly on his navy blue uniform jacket, it was also on the arm facing away from the door, so John had not noticed it. The guard went down the platform, slamming all the doors of the train, he then blew his whistle, waved his green flag and the train slowly pulled out of the station. The two servicemen gazed at the damage that was visible from the window of the train. It gradually gathered speed, and in a few minutes the scene changed and the damaged buildings gave way to green fields. Chris plucked up courage to speak to John, he gave a little cough: "Er, I see you've had a bereavement. Was it by any chance … er … was it to do wi' t' bombardment?" John just nodded. "Aye, me too. Me family, me Mam and Dad and me brothers." John gasped, he had heard of the family that had been wiped out. "Oh you poor chap, that makes my loss seem insignificant by comparison. My fiancée was killed. We were to have been married last week." Bonded by their common grief, the two men talked about their bereavements until the train drew in to York station. They discovered that they were both heading for the same destination, London, so having changed at York they continued their journey together. They found some comfort in being able to talk to each other, and share their grief, comparative strangers with a common feeling. At King's Cross, they parted company after exchanging home and service addresses. Chris gave Cissie's as his home address, he had no idea what was to happen to the family home, neither did he care, he had no intention of ever living there again. His one thought now was to get back on active service and somehow, he did not yet know how he was to achieve it, but somehow, avenge the deaths of his family.

117

Julia finally broached the subject of Audrey's future. She suggested that her sister-in-law might like to come and live with her in Manchester. She was surprised but secretly relieved when Audrey firmly declined. During the last few days Julia had been amazed at the change in her brother's widow. Audrey had always seemed to be a clingy sort of woman, very dependent on her husband and very devoted to him. Since Christmas she seemed to have found a hidden strength.

"No," she said firmly in answer to Julia's proposal, "thank you for thinking of it, Julia, but I would rather stay here." Audrey paused as tears came to her eyes, she swallowed, trying to compose herself. "I need to be near Geoffrey," she went on, "I need to be able to visit his grave. Jasper would rather be here too, I know there are parks in Manchester, but it wouldn't be the same as being able to run about on the sands and on the cliffs."

"I understand," Julia replied gently, "I understand, dear, but you will come and visit me from time to time won't you?"

"Yes, of course, and you will come as usual during the school holidays." They embraced as they settled their immediate future, but Julia wondered if Audrey would really be able to cope on her own without her beloved Geoffrey.

118

On the surface, the town was getting back to normal after the trauma of the bombardment and the celebration of Christmas. The debris was slowly being cleared, but many people were still homeless. Friends and relatives took in some until their own homes were habitable again or until they could find somewhere else to live. Others were in temporary, makeshift accommodation until the Town Council could re-house them. The propaganda posters and the sense of outrage had been instrumental in creating an upsurge of young men patriotically volunteering to join the army and the navy, much to the distress of their wives and mothers. Those who lived through that day in December 1914 always remembered; it changed the lives of so many people. Iris lived until her mid nineties; she became very confused in her later years and forgot many things, but the events of the bombardment remained forever clear in her mind. She talked about it often, and wondered what had happened to her shoe!

The New Year would soon begin, it should have brought new hope, but instead it only brought more horror, more sorrow, and more distress, as the "war to end all wars" progressed.

POSTSCRIPT

Many decades after the bombardment a publication by the Imperial War Museum showed that the bombardments of Scarborough, Whitby and Hartlepool could have been avoided.

The Admiralty discovered on December 14th 1914 that a German cruiser squadron was set to sail early the following morning, Tuesday December 15th returning in the evening of December 16th. An Admiralty signal to Admiral Sir John Jellicoe Commander of the fleet said: "The enemy will have time to reach our coast. Send at once, leaving tonight, the battle cruiser squadron and light squadron supported by a battle squadron. At dawn on Wednesday (December 16th December) they should be at some point where they can intercept the enemy on his return"

The gamble failed. The Admiralty's priority was to annihilate the attackers on their return rather than prevent the attacks on Scarborough, Whitby and Hartlepool. A series of blunders and a change for the worse in the weather enabled the German warships to escape.

First Sea Lord Fisher and Admiral Jellicoe were furious. It took a while for the Admiralty to get their revenge. The Von der Tann and the Derfflinger were damaged at the Battle of Jutland by the Royal Navy in 1916 and were finally scuttled by their own crews at Scapa Flow in May 1919 in protest against of the Versailles Peace agreement.

Admiral Jellicoe was granted honorary freedom of Scarborough in May 1928. In a speech in the Council Chamber he blamed the bad weather for the hampering the Royal Navy's mission without referring to the prior knowledge of the attack. If this prior knowledge had been acted on, over one hundred and twenty lives in three towns could have been saved.